James Payn

Fallen Fortunes

Vol. 3

James Payn

Fallen Fortunes
Vol. 3

ISBN/EAN: 9783337047467

Printed in Europe, USA, Canada, Australia, Japan

Cover: Foto ©Andreas Hilbeck / pixelio.de

More available books at **www.hansebooks.com**

FALLEN FORTUNES.

A Novel.

BY

JAMES PAYN,

AUTHOR OF "LOST SIR MASSINGBERD," "WALTER'S WORD," ETC.

In Three Volumes.

VOL. III.

London:

TINSLEY BROTHERS, 8, CATHERINE STREET, W.C.

1876.

CHARLES DICKENS AND EV.
CRYSTAL PALACE PRESS.

CONTENTS.

FALLEN FORTUNES.

CHAPTER I.

A CATASTROPHE.

"Oh Mamma! Kitty! news, news!" cried Tony, running joyfully into his mother's room one morning. She was not yet up; yielding to her daughters' entreaties and to the monitions of her own growing sense of weakness, she had of late consented to take her morning meal in her bed-room.

As her son entered, she rose from the pillow with eager eyes.

"What news, my child? It is not post-time yet. How *can* there be news?"

Kitty too, who was arranging some late autumn flowers in a little vase upon the dressing-table, so that her mother should see them reflected in the glass, turned round with a beating heart. "The ship must have arrived at Rio!" thought she.

"Oh mamma!" said Tony, his ardour greatly cooled, and half-conscious of having aroused undue expectations, "the first snow has fallen upon the fell. It is quite high up; but one can see it plainly, and it looks so beautiful. Margate says that it will not go away again till late in the spring; and that its coming so early is a sign of a hard winter. What is the matter, dear mamma?"

Mrs. Dalton had sunk back on the pillow, and covered her face with her thin hands. What sort of news she had expected, Kitty knew not; but it was plain that the disappointment had been a terrible blow.

"A hard winter," she repeated, "a hard winter."

"That is what Margate says," continued Tony, reassuringly; "but Margate may not be right, you know. And even if she is, what will it matter? The snow will fall and fall; the beck will be frozen; the roads will be choked up, so that only light carts can come; and we shall be snug and cosy in Sanbeck, all by ourselves, just as though we were out of the world."

"Out of the world," repeated his mother slowly.

"Yes, mamma; but why should *we* care, being all together," reasoned Tony gently. "I have heard you say yourself, that you are always happy when you have us about you; and I am so glad that I am not at Eton this half."

She was kissing him now in a strange, passionate manner, and the rare tears were streaming down her cheeks. Kitty would have drawn the boy away; but she signed to her to leave him.

"You have not forgotten who is *not* here amongst us all, Tony?" whispered she.

"Oh no, mamma: I often think of dear papa."

"And pray for him, darling? Do you pray for him?"

"Yes, indeed I do; every night and morning," answered he in her ear, "just as you taught me. There is no snow where he is gone, Jenny says. —I went to Jenny first, because I knew she was up and at her desk. And I have promised her to write to him all about it. Margate says there will be skating on the mere, and sleighing; the timber trucks make capital sleighs, and the boys will draw me—half-a-dozen of them at a time, Margate says—and one shoots down the fell like an arrow. Now, all that will be something to write about to papa. I don't mind writing, when I have got something to write about—that's *her* difficulty, Jenny says; so it happens to clever people as well as to stupid ones. And oh, dear mamma, I do hope you will get out as far as the bridge to-day, and see the snow on the fell."

Poor Tony came back to that as his one strong point, and the sole excuse for his enthusiasm; but he felt that it was not so strong as it was, and that he had overrated the importance of his tidings. He even understood that his mother's thoughts were too occupied with "dear papa" to take much interest in the natural phenomenon which had taken place; but beyond that, matters were a puzzle to him. Kitty, on the other hand, now felt that Jenny had been right when she said that her mother suspected something was amiss; that her apprehensions respecting the *Flamborough Head* and the precious life it carried were not less poignant than hers and Jenny's, though they had not the same sad foundation. She had never said one word to her of her walk to the mere with Uncle George, or even referred to his visit; a suspicious circumstance of itself, and which, joined

to what she had seen that morning, made tender
Kitty's heart bleed.

Jenny had now no secrets from her sister as
respected the steamer. Jeff had written again—
at Jenny's desire—describing what had happened
at Lloyd's; how first "the Committee" had announced "that they would be glad of information
regarding the *Flamborough Head*," and how afterwards it had been placed in the dread list of
"Missing Vessels." Yet even he had not said one
word of the paragraph about the wreck, wishing
to spare his correspondent, and ignorant that ill
news was already known.

So week after week went by, and the snow fell
as Margate had prophesied it would do—heavier
than it had been known to fall for many a year in
Sanbeck; no roll of wheel nor beat of hoof was
heard—and indeed, save the doctor's pony and
the butcher's light cart from Bleabarrow (the latter
only at long intervals), there was no traffic of any
kind in the little valley. The voice of its stream
was hushed, and its fir-trees, too heavily weighted
by the snow, had ceased to murmur; all was silence
and solitude. The Daltons were literally out of
the world. Few letters arrived for them now,
even when the postman came, which was not always

(for there was danger of him being "smoored" in
the drifts); the most sympathising folks cannot be
always writing to condole with us, and there was
no opportunity, alas! in this case for aught else
but condolence. Our misfortunes are wearisome
to our friends as well as ourselves, and make
dumb both us and them. As to the Daltons' ordinary acquaintances, who had been very numerous,
the family had "gone under," and were already
forgotten. Kitty was the one who suffered most
from this isolation; to her mother it seemed well
to be alone with her wretchedness; and Jenny
had Occupation—the balm for anxious minds.
She was for ever writing and reading. Kitty was
fond of reading, but not of study: she was not
omnivorous, like her sister, and the library of the
late Mr. Landell had few attractions for her. She
was, in truth, a devotee at the shrine of the cir-
culating library; a persecuted faith, but one which
has a great many charming followers. As the
family subscription in London was not yet run
out, the books came down with those of the
Campdens to Riverside, and were afterwards forwarded by carrier.

"If the snow permits it, pray send me over our
batch of books," wrote Kitty imploringly to Mary;

" it is a case of real destitution ; I am starving for light literature : not a novel has met my eye for a fortnight. I am now reading the ' Pilgrim's Progress '—the most recent work in the library of the Nook."

Mrs. Campden denounced this note as "flippant," considering the circumstances of Kate's position. The writer, indeed, was by no means in a flippant mood ; only she no longer wore her heart upon her sleeve with respect to Mary. She did not feel inclined to lay bare to her her miserable anxieties, and affected a gaiety that she was far enough from feeling. It is true we should never affect anything ; but Kitty would have found it hard to please Mrs. Campden now by any style of composition. With a large class of persons, the unfortunate, like the absent, are always in the wrong ; and besides, the mistress of Riverside was angry with the girl for refusing or withholding encouragement to Mr. Holt.

However, the books were sent off as requested, and reached their destination, although with some difficulty, and not until late in the afternoon. The carrier, who was suitably entertained in the kitchen by Margate, in recompense for his courage, gave a terrible account of his journey. If his cart had

not been the best built and lightest of all carts,
and the horse a paragon of strength and endurance,
he could never have come up the valley! The
snow was five or six feet deep in many places, and
hung so heavy on the hedge-rows that they looked
like white walls! He tossed off his glass of spirits
so quickly after his meal, in order that he might
get home before dark, that he found he had just
time for another. The treasure he had brought
with him was taken into the parlour, and at once
divested by Kitty of its coverings. She had
thrown down the brown paper and the white upon
the ground, and plunged in a first volume of her
favourite author; and under his benign influence
Time, notwithstanding its weight and weariness
and woe, was flying. She only knew that it was
growing late because of the waning light, which
made her bring the enchanted pages nearer to the
window. Presently, her mother entered the room,
and her first act was to pick up the discarded
wrappings of the parcel.

"Oh mamma, I am *so* sorry," said Kate, re-
morsefully. Neither she nor her sister, though
neat enough in their personal appearance, were
tidy; whereas, if Mrs. Dalton had a weakness,

beside good-will for everybody, it was for putting things straight.

"Nay, nay, my dear," answered she smiling; "don't reproach yourself: it was natural enough that, in your eagerness for the kernel you should forget the husk."

"But that I should have made you stoop to pick them up, mamma—I am quite ashamed of myself."

And she cheerfully shut up her book with the air of a good nun, who has prescribed for herself a penance.

"Nay, my darling; I am going to look through our weekly accounts; so do not punish yourself in that way. I don't want you to make yourself agreeable just now; only please to get the lamp, for my old eyes will not serve me in this twilight."

Neither Margate nor her myrmidon was entrusted with the trimming of the lamp, which, with many another household duty, was now Kitty's peculiar care. Notwithstanding the economical fashion in which the Daltons lived at the Nook—it was much more meagre than what fine folk call "quiet"—their establishment was to be even still more reduced; it was found that Lucy could

not be retained beyond the quarter. The fact
was, with all their good sense and wish to spend
as little as possible, certain free-handed habits—a
shilling here and sixpence there, and food for
whoever set foot in the house on real or pretended
service—could not be discarded all on a sudden.
In vain the weekly accounts were pared to the
thinnest proportions; the "extras" somehow swal-
lowed up the savings. Of course it would be a
pang to part with their last attendant; but not so
severe as it would have been a few weeks ago.
Although her emoluments were the same as
before, Lucy was not so easily reconciled to the
roughness of the new régime as were her mistress
and the young ladies; and she complained of the
lack of "society." Margate's gossip—for it is not
to be supposed that Nature had denied her the
usual springs of conversation—itself by no means
piquant, was also entirely local; while "the gurl,"
as the third retainer of the family was scornfully
denominated by the lady's-maid, was a mere sponge
or sucker. Her ears—and mouth—were open for
everything, but there was no reciprocity. We
cannot all of us be self-denying for ever; it is
something if one makes a temporary sacrifice at

the shrine of duty, and poor Lucy had found by
this time that her promise of life-long service to
her old employers would be not a little irksome to
keep. So she was parting from them, though on
the best of terms; and in the meantime Kitty was
learning to "make herself useful" about the house
—a very elastic phrase, which, as we have seen,
included lamp-trimming. A neater-handed Phyllis
than Kitty it is impossible to imagine; and whatever she set her hand to she graced. If you could
have seen her now, as she comes up the oaken
stair with the lamp, burnished, and throwing its
mellow light upon her golden hair, you would
have said that the Daltons had one family ornament at least still left to them, one rare and
beautiful picture, which — however humble its
frame—would not escape the judicious eye of the
connoisseur.

"Congratulate me, mamma, upon my success,"
said she, as she stepped carefully into the parlour
over the raised threshold that had been very
literally a stumbling-block from generation to
generation of the dwellers in the Nook. "Does
it not burn well?"

There was no reply; and, hastily setting down

the lamp, Kitty looked around her in some tre-
pidation. Under the deep window-seat where she
had herself been sitting a few minutes before, lay
a motionless figure.

"Mamma!" shrieked she, in an agony, and was
down on her knees beside her in a second; then
"Lucy! Margate! Help! help!" rang through
the old house.

Her first thought was of physical aid, and
therefore she did not call Jenny; yet Jenny arrived
somehow—though her chamber was farthest off—
as soon as the others. When the kitchen-girl,
rushing in with the rest, wrung her hands and
cried, "She is dead, she is dead!" it was Jenny
who said, "Hush, fool!" as Margate afterwards
observed, "like a man," and took the direction of
affairs.

"Lift her up and put her on the sofa," was the
order that three pair of strong and willing arms
promptly obeyed; and in the meantime, Jenny's
own hands had removed the pillow.

"She has fainted; that is all, Jenny," whispered Kitty, with anxious pleading.

"How did it happen? Where did you find
her?" returned the other, in the same low
voice.

"Just as you saw her. I had left the room for the lamp, only a minute or two."

"What is that newspaper in the corner?"

"It is what the books were wrapped in; mamma has just taken them up."

Jenny walked quickly forward and picked up the paper. Her eye, glancing quickly over the page, fell at once on the heading: "Supposed loss of the *Flamborough Head.*" "Good God, Kitty, mamma has read it—the paragraph about the wreck. Margate, some one must go for Dr. Curzon instantly; not one moment is to be lost."

"Indeed, ma'am, there is not a soul to send. If we had known it before the carrier had gone; but there is not a man nearer than Farmer Boynton's; and the snow——"

"I will go," cried a small voice, half-choked with tears; and Tony, who had crept in unobserved, and was standing by his mother's side in a passion of silent grief, instantly left the room, and the next moment was seen flying across the courtyard.

"The poor child has not even put on his cloak," murmured Margate, pitifully. The night was falling, and the snow was deep; but at that awful time, with that lifeless form and death-like face lying before them, neither Kitty nor Jenny could think of aught save her who had given them being.

CHAPTER II.

AT nine years old some town-boys are already men in matters upon which a large class of men most pride themselves : in self-reliance, habits of economy, and the art, if not of getting on in the world, at all events of taking good care of themselves in it. In seven years more, if such a lad is in the coster-monger line, he will even have a wife and a carriage. But in the upper classes, our boys remain boys for a long time—some of them, under exceptionally favourable circumstances, even all their lives—and notwithstanding the boasted advantages of our public schools, are strangely helpless and dependent. They are trusted early enough (occasionally too early) to go to the play by themselves with a sovereign in their pocket ; but without the sovereign—without, that is to say, the adventitious aids, and claims upon the services of others, to which they have always

been accustomed—the British school-boy is no match
for the street Arab of one-half his years. When
Master Anthony Dalton set out on his errand to
Dr. Curzon's, he had not even "the light heart and
the thin pair of breeches" so much eulogised by
philosophers as adapted to the needs of human
life. He had a very heavy heart and knicker-
bockers. There was nothing on the side of this
gallant young gentleman, aged nine, but pluck
and a good cause; and there were a great many
things—including the wind, which was from the
north-west, and blew right up the valley—against
him.

Like the rest of his race, he was of delicate constitution, and had been brought up delicately, as
was natural enough in a family in which he was
the only boy. Town-born and town-bred, he had
never even seen the country save in summer-time,
till he came to the Nook, and had probably never
been out in it, save in a carriage, after dark. He
was not the least of a "molly-coddle," and certainly
no coward; yet if the road to Dr. Curzon's had been
throughout in its normal state, and well lit as a
London street, circumstances had been such with
Tony as to render his present expedition, in the
phrase of his women-folk, "quite an undertaking;"

and considering that the night soon grew to be so
dark that he could scarcely see a yard before him,
and that the snow was everywhere two feet deep at
least in the roadway, and sometimes half-a-dozen, it
must be allowed that the child had his work before
him. Of difficulty, however, and far less of danger,
Tony had no thought as he ran down the noiseless
road towards the bridge. His mind was full of his
mother, the sight of whose death-like features had
appalled him, and his one consuming idea was to
bring Dr. Curzon to her side and save her life. He
no longer sobbed, but husbanded his breath for her
dear sake, and plied his little legs. It had been his
intention at first to go to Farmer Boynton's as
Margate had suggested, and get a messenger from
among the men at the homestead; but the farm was
some way up the valley, in the contrary direction to
the doctor's house, and he felt that time would be
lost by his so doing. If he could fetch the doctor
himself—and the snow was not very deep as yet,
though he made but slow progress—help would
reach the Nook all the sooner. Behind were the
lights of the village; on the left was the solitary
beacon of Boynton's farm; to the right lay the
long road, so white and yet so dark, with no glimmer
from house or homestead; yet to the right he

turned, and plunged on through the half-yielding
snow.

It was a pitiful struggle, as struggles against
Nature in her iron mood mostly are; and the odds,
always great against poor humanity, were in this
case overwhelming. The little lad did not even
know, what any child who does "the wheel" for
halfpence from the knife-board, could have told him,
how to husband his breath. He was almost "pumped
out" already, yet he ran on at the top of his speed.
It was grown too dark to distinguish the hard snow
from that which was rotten and gave way to his
light tread, or to avoid the deep furrows left by the
carrier's cart. A slight bend of the road had
already hidden the lights behind him, and walls of
snow shut him in to right and left. His mind re-
verted to a picture in the old house at home of the
retreat from Moscow, of a young conscript left behind by his comrades, and perishing in the white
and solitary waste. It had taken hold of his childish
imagination, and he had often dreamt of it in his
little cot, and been glad to wake in the morning
and find his mother's face looking down upon him
with her sweet smile. At that recollection his
heart smote him for having forgotten the condition
in which he had left her, even for a moment, and

he sped on with renewed vigour. If will could have done it, Tony would have run on to York, had it been necessary; but unhappily it is not true that wherever there is a will there is a way. The boy began to stumble, and then to stagger, like a drunken man. His legs still moved, but mechanically; he had lost control over them, and was presently landed, head first, in a snowdrift by the wayside; there he lay for a few seconds, half unconscious. He would have been glad enough to remain there for ever, but the thought of his mother still spurred him on, and he contrived to extricate himself. There was a sharp pain in his right foot, as though a hot iron had seared it; his shoe had come off in the snow. As he ran on, he sent forth one wild passionate cry—a bitter acknowledgment of failure, rather than an appeal for aid; then stumbled and fell.

"Hulloa! there; hulloa!" responded a gruff voice. Tony heard it, but as one hears a voice in dreams.

"I say, hulloa!" continued the voice reproachfully, as though a civil observation of that description, civilly put, had deserved a civil reply. Then the light of a lantern gleamed over the track, and John Bates, the Bleabarrow carrier, came cautiously along it, and almost fell over the boy's prostrate body. Then he exclaimed " Hulloa !" again, but this time in a very astonished tone—it was a word he had evidently found capable of great modulation —and stooping down, picked up poor Tony.

"Why, hulloa ! young gentleman "—here the word expressed commiseration as well as surprise —" this is a pretty game, especially played with 'one shoe off and one shoe on,' like 'my man John' our Emmy sings about. It's my opinion as it's precious lucky for thee that the old mare came to a full stop just where she did, or thou wouldst never have seen the Nook again." He carried the boy back to his cart, which was stuck fast in the snow, a few yards ahead, and placed him tenderly among some empty sacks.

" Well, this settles me not to try to push on any more.—Coom, Ned, coom " (here he addressed his horse) ; " let us turn round and go back to San-beck."

" The doctor, the doctor ! " cried Tony, suddenly, raising himself from the sacks. " Mamma's ill, and wants the doctor."

" And could they find nobody in all the place but a little lad like thee to fetch the doctor to thy mother such a night as this ? "

"Yes; a man could have gone from Farmer Boynton's, but I thought I could go quicker myself. Oh, please let us go at once."

"But the wheels can't move a yard that way; and I doubt whether I could get there afoot myself. To be sure, I could take Ned out, and ride him, and leave thee here in the cart."

"I said I would fetch the doctor," said Tony, resolutely, "and I'd rather do it."

"Very good; and so thou shalt. With thy bare foot, and in such sad plight, it will be better for thee to be put to bed at Dr. Curzon's. So, I will ride Ned, and take thee before me. If it had not been for the good stuff they gave me at the Nook, I should been starved o' cold by this time; and one good turn deserves another."

The honest carrier needed not have thus found an excuse for an act of benevolence which was natural to him. Most men who pass their lives exposed to wind and weather have wholesome natures. The possession of an "Emmy" of his own, too, doubtless made "the soft spot" in Mr. John Bates's heart still softer. He unharnessed the horse; and throwing a sack or two on his bare back, for Tony's accommodation, mounted, and placing the boy before him, moved slowly along

the snow-choked way towards the doctor's house.
They reached it at last, taking six times the time
they would have done upon ordinary occasions;
and scarcely less astonished was the worthy doctor
at their appearance than if they had been two
veritable Knights Templars, travelling according
to the ancient custom of their order. He looked
grave, indeed, when Tony told him his errand;
but reassuming his habitual cheerfulness, at once
ordered his pony to be brought round.

"As for you, young gentleman, since you have
lost a shoe," said he, "you had better sleep at my
house."

But Tony besought so earnestly to be taken
back to the Nook, to see about mamma, that
having been fortified as to his inward boy with
something hot, and wrapped up in various warm
coverings, he was once more placed before the
carrier, who had made up his mind to stay the
night at Farmer Boynton's; and the three started
together for Sanbeck. It was an expedition that
in after-years Tony never forgot, down to its
minutest details; the great events of human life
stamp not only themselves upon the mind, but
all the surroundings which accompany them: the
snow-clad road, the leaden night, and every incident

of his noiseless journey, were destined to hang in that picture-gallery of the past (which there are none so poor as not to possess) for ever; the very motion of the sturdy shoulders of the horse the boy so unwontedly bestrode, recurred to him long after his two companions had paid the debt of nature.

Though they rode through the muffled court-yard of the Nook without a sound, the servant-girl, who was on the watch, ran out to meet them, and whispered something in the doctor's ear; he was off his pony in an instant, but not before Tony had scrambled down from his huge steed.

" No, my boy," said the doctor, gravely, as the lad was about to limp upstairs; " you must not go to your mamma's room just now."

" What is the matter, Sue ? Is mamma worse?" cried Tony, wildly; his little legs trembled under him with fatigue and apprehension of he knew not what. The girl picked him up in her strong arms, and placed him in a chair by the kitchen fire.

" No, no ; now the doctor has come all will be right," said she; " but you must not run about without your shoes. What a walk you must have had through the snow and dark ! "

"Oh, that's nothing; at least, nothing to cry about;" for the girl had begun to sob hysterically. "Tell me about mamma."

A thin, shrill, quavering cry was heard above-stairs.

"What is that, Sue?"

"You have got a little baby brother, Master Tony; such a dear little thing!"

Tony was nonplussed. He had always understood that the doctors brought these little strangers; but if Dr. Curzon had brought this one, he must have carried it in the crown of his hat—a performance Tony had never seen equalled save by a conjurer in London, who had brought a bowl of gold-fish out of the same receptacle.

"I should like to see my baby brother, if I can't see mamma," said Tony, dreamily; he had but a faint interest in this newly-arrived relative, and he felt dreadfully tired.

"So you shall, if you will just lie down in your bed a bit: it *is* your bedtime nearly, and you *must* take off your wet things, you know."

"But you'll call me directly mamma asks to see me?" pleaded the boy.

"Oh yes, Master Tony, yes; when she asks, I

will." There was something strange in the girl's voice and manner, which he could not understand. But he was too worn out for guessing riddles. He even submitted to be carried into his own little room, an indignity he had not endured for many a year, and was put to bed like a child, or a gentleman who has taken too much champagne.

In the morning he awoke so late that the sun was streaming full upon his bed, and upon Jenny's thin, white face, who was bending over his pillow with an expression that he had never seen her wear before: it was tender, but yet grave and almost stern.

" Have I overslept myself, Jenny, and got late for lessons ? " said he. Then rapidly collecting his ideas : " And how is mamma? Sue promised that when she asked for me—— Oh Jenny, what is the matter ? "

" Mamma will never ask for you again, dear Tony, nor for any of us. She is——"

" Dead ? " The boy burst into passionate sobs. " Oh, don't say dead, Jenny ! "

" Yes, darling. We have lost the best mother that ever children had."

"Oh mamma, mamma!" cried Tony, stretching out his little arms. It was terrible to see so young a creature so torn with anguish.

The door opened, and Kitty entered, her beautiful face puckered with weeping. "You have told him, then, Jenny?" said she, in broken tones.

"Yes, dear; I thought it best."

"But why, *why* did they not send for me? Why did they let me sleep?" asked Tony, reproachfully. "Did mamma never ask——"

"Yes, darling, yes," said Kitty; "she did ask for you, but not in time; and when we told her you had gone for the doctor, through the dark and snow, she thanked you with her sweet eyes. 'My poor, poor boy,' she said. It is we who are to be pitied, darling, and not she, for she is an angel in heaven."

"Sue told me I had a baby brother?" said Tony, softly, after a little pause.

"Yes, dear, you have."

"How strange and sad it will be for poor papa," continued the boy, thoughtfully, "to hear that mamma has gone to heaven, and that there is a baby brother!"

Neither Kitty nor Jenny could make reply.

They had not the heart to tell him that in all human probability the news that had broken their mother's heart was true; that they three—and the baby boy—were left alone in the world; not only motherless, but fatherless.

CHAPTER III.

BEREAVED.

WHAT change happens to those who have cast off this mortal coil, He only knows who has put it for a brief span upon us; but it can hardly be much greater than that which befalls the living whom the beloved ones have left behind them.

> To know they have departed,
> Their voice, their face, are gone;
> To feel impatient-hearted,
> Yet know we must live on,

is an experience that transcends all others in this world. The vacant chair in the household that has been knit together in bonds of love, has all the sacredness of the altar, and ten times its suggestiveness. For the time it seems as though the sun had vanished from the skies and all was dark. The home has lost its charm, and is more hateful, because more full of bitterest remindings, than any stranger's roof. We weep, we plead, we beat against the gates of heaven, to call the lost one back—in vain. What is wealth, or health, compared with that which yesterday we thought but a common blessing, taken as a matter of course, treated as though it would remain with us for ever, and now is gone! Oh cruel Fate! unpitying Arbiter! Oh Worker of Desolation and Despair!

> 'Tis better to have loved and lost,

says one,

> Than never to have loved at all.

It may be so, but that is too hard a saying for us even to understand, much more to derive comfort from it; for the love of the departed one was a portion of our very selves, the spring of our every action, the theme of our deepest thought—and he has left us for ever. It is idle to tell us we shall meet again. What consolation is it to the child who weeps and clings, when sent from home for the first time to school, that there will be holidays at midsummer! And we are in worse plight than he, for we are not sure—the very best of us are not quite sure—that there *will* be holidays. And if there be, what change will not be wrought

in us. We may be children then no more; and
he too that has gone before may be unrecog-
nisable. " Death is common." " All is for
the best." " It is the will of God." Cold comfort all.

Think of the Nook in Sanbeck, with the snow
without, and the pale corpse within; the orphaned
girls and Tony, well-nigh penniless, well-nigh
friendless, with their helpless charge, but one
day old. There are tens of thousands in the
land in worse plight than they; and tens of hundreds, rich in this world's goods, who complain
that they have no object in life, and devote themselves to Ritualism, Exeter Hall preachings, or old
china, in default of it.

The man who had killed Mrs. Dalton was poor
Mr. Marks the butler at Riverside, who had
thoughtlessly wrapped around Mr. Mudie's books
that fatal *Times*; but he was, after all, but the
immediate cause of her decease; she would have
died any way—so Dr. Curzon said—in bringing
that new life into the world. For weeks she
had dragged on with a breaking heart; consumed
with unutterable apprehensions upon her husband's account; uncheered by hope; and laden
with anxieties for her children's future. " If she

ain't gone to heaven, sir," observed old Margate in confidence to Dr. Curzon, "there ain't no such a place." An observation worth a good many beaten-out and attenuated remarks to the same effect which were made by others on the occasion.

They laid her in the sunniest spot of the little God's-acre—the purest embodiment of good it had ever known—and many a genuine tear was dropped for her from eyes unused to pay such tribute. Dr. Curzon was deeply affected, and Mr. Campden also. Kind Jeff, whose coming down from town for such a purpose was stigmatised by a certain lady as ' a most ridiculous act of extravagance," was among the mourners, and wept almost as bitterly as little Tony himself. The two girls accompanied the body to the grave, as likewise did Mrs. Campden and her daughter.

"I would go much farther than to Sanbeck churchyard," said the former, " to show my respect for the memory of dearest Edith ; " and there is no reason to doubt her word, though there would probably have been limits as to distance.

She meant to be kind after her fashion, but she was certainly not judicious in entering as she did upon the material aspect of their affairs

with the poor mourners on the very day on
which their mother had been laid in her grave.
Her daughter and herself had returned with them
to the Nook after the funeral; while her husband
and the doctor, with Jeff and Tony, were taking a
walk towards the mere, which the melting of the
snow during the previous week—one of sunshine
and comparative mildness—enabled them to do.
"It is so much more easy for men to escape from
disagreeable scenes than women," as Mrs. Campden
justly observed; although she might have added
that certain scenes disagreeable to all men are not
so to all women. We do not mean to say that
Mrs. Campden absolutely enjoyed her visit to the
Nook upon the present melancholy occasion, but
without doubt it had some pleasing features for
her. It was an occasion that—in many senses—
could be improved, and she was fond of improv-
ing an occasion. Without exactly putting herself
in the place of the girls' "natural protector"—
which would have involved something beside
privileges—she was in an undeniable position
for offering advice, if not for absolute dictation;
and for playing the patroness as far as that game
could be played for love. As their only kins-
woman, she had really succeeded to some authority

over them, and Kitty, at least, was willing to admit it.

"My dear girls," said she impressively, "you have a right to look to me in future—for counsel; and, God willing, it shall never be denied you. Your dear mother's death has in no respect altered your position in my affections, unless it be to make you dearer to me. I am sure my Mary feels the same."

"Kitty and Jenny both know that, mamma, without my telling them," said Mary brusquely. She had a consciousness, quickened by a certain expression in Jenny's eye, that this speech of her mother's was not quite what it should be, or, at all events, that it was not very warmly appreciated.

"My dear child, in a solemn hour like this, one should not only think, but speak, the words of cheer. It has pleased an inscrutable Providence to deprive your cousins of their natural guardian; indeed, there is only too much reason to fear of *both* their parents. They are, unhappily, also left but slenderly provided for. Under these circumstances, it behoves those who love them to speak with tenderness, yet with decision. It is impossible at their age that they should know the world, or what is

best for them to do in the world; and it is my
duty to tell them that in reality their choice is very
small. Even with the experience of their good
mother to aid them, they have found it hard, I
fear, to make both ends meet; and they will find
it still harder now."

"Do you call these 'words of cheer,' madam?"
inquired Jenny, suddenly, with the air of a person
who asks for information.

"They are words of truth, at all events, my
poor girl," answered Mrs. Campden, pityingly,
"as you will surely discover; though, indeed,
I was not addressing myself so much to you as
to Kate. Well, in this your extremity, as I may
truly call it, a friend has unexpectedly proffered
his aid."

"Mr. Holt, I suppose?" said Jenny, coldly.

"Yes, it *is* Mr. Holt, Jane; though I don't
know why you should suppose any such thing,"
answered Mrs. Campden, reprovingly. "You have
no claim upon his good offices, so far as I know,
in any way. Yet only consider what he has done.
From the moment that that dreadful paragraph
appeared in the newspaper which has already
worked such woe—poor Marks is quite broken-
hearted about his share in the matter, and I hope

it will be a lesson to him never to act without thought, as long as he lives—I say, ever since these miserable tidings came to England, Mr. Holt has been moving heaven and earth to get your father's insurance-money paid——"

Kitty started to her feet. "What! is there, then, no hope?" cried she.

Jenny trembled in every limb, but remained silent. Her courage was greater than that of her sister, but her strength was small.

"I fear that there is very little hope, Kitty," said Mrs. Campden, quietly. "We must not disguise from ourselves what has really happened. The ship is many weeks behind its time, and has been already 'written off'—I believe that is the phrase—at Lloyd's; and then there is this shattered boat picked up belonging to it. The *Flamborough Head* is painted on it. Nothing can be more morally conclusive. On the other hand, there is a difficulty about the payment of your father's insurance by the *Palm Branch*, because his death cannot be substantiated. Mr. Campden could tell you all about it, because he is a director of the Company, but he naturally feels a delicacy in talking of it. From his very connection with the matter, his lips are in a manner sealed."

"Why?" inquired Jenny.

"My good girl, I wish you would not speak so brusquely. It is positively startling. You must really get out of that curt manner, which is the reverse of conciliatory. Of course I don't mind it myself, that is to say seriously—but others may take objection to it; and under present circumstances it behoves you to make no enemies, but all the friends you can. The reason is surely evident enough why my husband, being a director, and indeed the chairman of the *Palm Branch,* can take no steps that may prejudice its interests on behalf of a personal friend. The Company has for the present refused to pay, and in the meantime money will be wanting to you for a hundred things—for what has happened to-day, for one. Forgive me for alluding to matters that must needs give you pain; but this is no time for false delicacy. Well, you want money at once, and for the present the *Palm Branch* will not pay the sum to which you would be entitled if the fact of your father's death could be established. Under these circumstances, the kind friend of whom I speak has offered to advance you whatever may be required."

"That is very generous," said Kitty, softly.

"The advance would be made on the security of the insurance," observed Jenny.

"Well, yes, of course it would. But if your father is alive the loan is lost, for where is he to find the money to repay it?"

"Then in that case Mr. Holt would be giving us the money, would he not?" continued Jenny.

"Yes, indeed; and there are very few persons, let me tell you, who would make so noble, so large-hearted an offer."

"Let us hope there would be also very few persons who would accept it, Mrs. Campden."

"Jane, you must be mad!" cried Mrs. Campden, angrily. "Kate, if you have any influence with your sister—for it seems I have none—I do trust you will exert it for her own benefit. She does not understand her position."

"You are wrong there, Mrs. Campden; thanks to your plain speaking—a duty, as you call it, in which you have never failed since our misfortunes began—it is quite impossible that any one of us could misunderstand it. Kitty, of course, will do as she thinks proper; but for myself I do not take one shilling of this man's money either as loan or gift. I would starve first."

"My dear Jenny!" cried Mary, with a little

scream; "pray don't say such dreadful things. Mamma always exaggerates, you know; things are not so bad——"

"Be quiet, Mary," interrupted Mrs. Campden, very sharply; "you are talking like a fool. If things are not so bad with your cousins, it is only in the sense that they are not so bad as they may be. It is impossible to imagine a darker future than awaits them, should they decline this opportune, and, I must say, most delicately offered aid. Fortunately, the decision does not rest with Jane, but with Kitty. She is the house manager, and knows how matters stand; and with the debt for her mother's very funeral hanging over her head——"

"Stop, stop!" pleaded Kitty, pitifully. "Do not talk of that to-day, I entreat you. Give me time—a few days at least—to think over what you have said, and then you shall have my answer."

"You will do as you please, my dear, of course," replied Mrs. Campden, with a pitying smile; "though why you should hesitate, even for a moment, is inexplicable to me. However, so be it. And now I have a proposition of my own to make, which has the merit, at all events"—here she threw a meaning glance at Jenny—"of being open to no misconstruction. It is my intention—for the present, at all events—to provide for the little baby. It is strong and healthy enough, Dr. Curzon says, notwithstanding its somewhat premature arrival, so that a wet nurse is as unnecessary as she would, under the circumstances, be unjustifiable; and our lodge-keeper's wife, Mrs. Hardy—who, it seems, had a great affection for its poor mother—has consented to take charge of it. We have plenty of cows, you know——"

"Oh, please, Mrs. Campden, I couldn't do that," interrupted Kitty, decisively. "The baby is the greatest comfort we have left to us. It is never out of my arms or Margate's, and she understands all about it quite as well as Mrs. Hardy. The milk is as good here, too, as at Riverside——"

"My dear child, that is not the question," put in the other, emphatically. "The question is, do you get the milk for nothing? Why, of course you don't; and therefore to keep the baby would be an act of extravagance."

"My dear mamma, I never heard of a baby being an article *de luxe*," said Mary, smiling.

"Very likely not; but your cousins are unfor-

tunately in a position to feel it as such," returned
her mother, gravely. "It is not as if you would be
separated from the child by any distance, Kitty;
and then, when you come over to Riverside, you
could always see it. And if it was seriously ill,
I should take care to let you know, of course."

Poor Kitty's face had been growing longer and
longer throughout this speech, for the baby was
inexpressibly dear to her, as well on its own account
as on that of her mother, of whom it seemed to
be a portion. Jenny could find forgetfulness of
her miseries in reading and writing; but for
herself, the soft, snoozie little form she rocked to
sleep upon her bosom was her only cure for the
heartache. When Mrs. Campden talked so calmly
of its being "seriously ill" miles away from her,
Kitty shuddered.

"Indeed, I could not part from the baby, Mrs.
Campden. It is almost the greatest treasure I
have left in life; and I don't think," added
she, with a faint smile, "it is a *very* expensive
luxury."

"You know your own affairs best, my dear,"
answered Mrs. Campden, coldly. "I meant nothing
but kindness by my offer." And she rose, and
pruned down her black silk and crape, in sign of

flight. "We have put up our horses at Farmer Boynton's, so that no unnecessary expense should be imposed on you; and I do hope you will be as considerate for yourself, Kitty, as your friends are for you. You understand what I mean. Now, I do trust to hear from you to-morrow or the next day, that your foolish scruples with respect to the offer of our common friend have been overcome." She kissed Kitty as she spoke; but Jenny had already betaken herself from the room, and Mrs. Campden perhaps was not displeased at the circumstance. She was not so indifferent to Jenny's brusqueness as she affected to be; the plain speaking on which she piqued herself was very unwelcome to her in others; and, besides, Jenny had a habit of quietly ripping up her satin speeches, and showing the seamy side of them, which made her particularly dislike that young lady. Of the baby, on the other hand, Mrs. Campden took a gracious leave—the woman's heart must be bad indeed that does not warm to a baby—and yet its infant charms by no means so intoxicated her as to warp her practical good sense.

"It's a dear little baby," said Mary; "is it not?" as she and her mother crossed the bridge towards the farm.

"Yes, indeed, and healthy too; though, under the circumstances, one can hardly wish that it should live."

"Fie, mamma, how you talk!" returned Mary, not a little shocked. It was creditable to her to have retained her susceptibilities so long; her mother's honest speech and high principles still gave her rather "a turn" occasionally.

"Well, the point is, what is the poor little creature to live *upon?*" returned the elder lady. "Even when Mr. Dalton's insurance-money is paid, there will hardly be enough for three mouths, much less for four. I suppose you don't wish your papa to be saddled with the maintenance of a *second* boy for all his life?"

"Well, that does seem hard upon us, certainly," answered Mary, her thoughts reverting to Jeff with some disfavour.

"Of course it would be hard—in fact, it is out of the question; and yet you say (rather disrespectfully, I must needs remark), 'How you talk, mamma!' when I say it is no charity to hope the child may live. If the carriage is ready, I shall not wait for your father. It will do him all the good in the world to walk home; and I am sure the accommodation at the farm is not at all what our horses are accustomed to."

In a few minutes the carriage drove by—close to the new-made grave—with the two ladies sitting in it alone.

CHAPTER IV.

MR. CAMPDEN was upon the whole not sorry to have been left behind by his wife in Sanbeck; the short way to Riverside over the crags was not, indeed, very nice walking in winter weather; but it was no great distance to Bleabarrow, where "the fly" could be procured to take him home; and he was really glad of being alone with Jeff, and of having a word or two in private with the two girls. Jeff had received no summons to Riverside upon this melancholy occasion—Mrs. Campden objected, as a matter of principle, to people running into expenses for mere sentiment—but had invited himself to Dr. Curzon's.

"I should like, if it would not be inconvenient to you," he wrote the doctor, "to pay the last tribute of respect to the best and dearest friend

I have had in the world;" and the doctor had allowed the plea, and welcomed the lad warmly.

He looked something more than a lad now; his life in town had given him an air of independence and self-possession, though without the least touch of conceit. He looked handsomer than ever, though his dark eyes were heavy with woe, and his fair face shadowed with grief, as he walked with little Tony ahead of their two companions, and talked in a low voice of the departed dear one.

With the squire and the doctor, as was natural, the future of the orphaned Daltons formed the chief topic of conversation; and in connection with it, Mr. Campden mentioned the offer that had been made by Mr. Holt.

"It was a deuced kind thing of the man, that I must say," observed he, when he had delivered this information, which he felt somehow had fallen flat.

"Very much so," said the doctor, "if it was disinterested."

"There was no promise attached to it whatsoever, my good friend; the offer was made quite free."

"Still, from what I have seen of Mr. Holt," persisted the other, "I should think he was a gentleman who looked, in some shape or another, for his *quid pro quo*. Moreover, I believe him clever enough to gauge the nature of those with whom he has to deal. If he lends our young friends money, he places them under an obligation; and there is only one way—as it seems to me—by which that obligation can be discharged."

"I think you are not very charitable to Mr. Holt," said Mr. Campden, with a little flush.

"Perhaps not," said the doctor drily. "Still, I think it hard upon the girl to place her in such a position. Suppose a lovely young woman, for example (and what can be more likely?), advanced *me* money upon very doubtful security—should not I be bound, if I could not repay her, to make her Mrs. C.?"

"I believe you're right, Curzon," said Mr. Campden suddenly; "it has struck me in the same light myself. The money, if they want it, shall be forthcoming some other way."

He gave a great sigh as he said that, as a thrifty man might do who has made up his mind to some extravagance; but Mr. Campden was not thrifty, and though he was counting the cost of what he had resolved to do, it was not the expense that made him sigh. If he advised the girls not to take

this money, especially if his wife had already persuaded them to do so, "there would be the deuce
of a row," he knew, with Julia.

"I say, Jeff, what is *your* opinion of Mr. Holt?"
inquired the doctor presently, pitching his voice so
as to reach the others; "that is, so far as you can
tell it consistently with loyalty to your chief."

"Ay, we mustn't disclose the secrets of the
prison-house, must we?" said Mr. Campden; "how
we rig the markets, and all that."

"I am bound to say that Mr. Holt has been
uniformly civil to me," replied the young fellow
frankly. "Nay, not only civil, but considerate. In
my ignorance and inexperience, I have no doubt
made lots of blunders in business matters, and he
has never said a word about them. And this is the
more creditable to him, because he hates me very
cordially, and he knows that I hate him."

"My dear Jeff, I am astonished at you!" exclaimed Mr. Campden. The doctor looked astonished too, but with a sly twinkle in his eyes that
did not speak reproof.

"No, sir; we don't like one another, and we
never shall," continued the young man; "but I
do my duty by him, I hope, and, as I say, I have
nothing to complain of in his behaviour to me."

"Well, I have known many partnerships carried on on worse terms," observed the doctor cheerfully. "But how was it that oil and vinegar were got to mix in the first instance?"

"The explanation is very simple, doctor. Mrs. Dalton—God bless her!—asked Mr. Holt to take me, and advised me to go. And—and—" here Jeff began for the first time to exhibit embarrassment—"nothing else happened to offer itself."

For the second time the colour came into Mr. Campden's face; he could not but remember the circumstances under which Jeff had been driven from Riverside. It was quite a relief to him that a bend of the road here showed them the village —they were now returning from the mere—and once more introduced, by association, the topic of the morning.

"I should like to have a few words with your sisters before I start, Tony," said the squire, "if they feel equal to see me."

"Oh, I am sure they would see *you*, Uncle George, because——" Here he stopped short; what he had in his mind was, "because they could see Mrs. Campden, who is not half so nice;" but unlike that lady, he sometimes felt a hesitation in speaking his mind.

"Because he is their best friend; eh, Tony?"
observed the doctor, hastening to the rescue.
"That is quite right. We three will take another
turn together while the squire goes in."

Since Mrs. Campden's departure that afternoon,
the two sisters had not met. Kitty had devoted
herself to the baby, and Jenny had remained in
her own room, endeavouring in vain to devote
herself to her books. They were both aware that
it behoved them to be doing *something* : not to
give themselves over to the grief that was impor-
tuning them to become its prey. They only
showed their weakness by avoiding the little
drawing-room when they conveniently could; since
it was there that the sense of loss oppressed them
most. The unfinished piece of work; the still
open desk; the book half read; the empty loung-
ing-chair, were for the present daggers, each of
which stabbed them to the very heart. Perhaps,
too, the consciousness of their disagreement—or
rather of their want of accord—with respect to
the proposition made by Mrs. Campden, had helped
to keep them apart for that half-hour or so. A
quarrel was impossible between them at any time,
much more on the very day when they had laid
in earth the being they had loved best upon it,

and who had repaid their love with such usurious
interest.   There were reasons, as I have shown,
why these two from the first should not have gone
the way of most sisters in this respect; and since
misfortune had befallen them, the bonds of love
between them had been naturally strengthened
and tightened. It is a poor fancy, indeed, that
has painted Love as flying out of the window when
Poverty knocks at the door. With those within,
if they be not utterly worthless, he remains a more
cherished guest than ever.   Indeed, it was only
their ordinary close affection and unanimity which
gave any importance to the difference of opinion
between the two sisters; it seemed so strange to
each that the other should take an opposite view of
any matter.

Jenny on her part had no doubt whatever as to
the course they were bound to follow with respect
to Mr. Holt's offer. If she had thought Kitty was
seriously thinking of accepting it, she would have
been furious.   She saw it at once in the very
light in which it appeared to Dr. Curzon. "This
impudent man was offering to lend his money upon
the very best of security—namely, on Kitty herself.
If the offer was accepted, it was in fact the offer of
his hand!" What hesitation, therefore, need there

be as to their reply? As to Mrs. Campden's making the proposition, that was only to be expected, after what had already happened, and was another reason, if such were wanted, for declining it. Sooner than see her Kitty sacrificed on the altar to Mammon, for the sake of herself and Tony and the baby, she *would* have " starved first."

But besides this bitter feeling, there was a fire kindled in Jenny's breast that flamed against almost everybody; nay, which resented the blows of Fate itself. She had taken it ill in church that day that the Bleabarrow clergyman—of whose cure Sanbeck formed a portion not much visited except in the summer months—should have spoken of her mother's future with charitable confidence. The words of Hamlet addressed to the officiating minister at Ophelia's grave would have expressed her thoughts. What priest on earth had the right to eulogise her mother, far less to hint a doubt of her perfection? As for the outside world, she scorned it; the chill touch of misfortune had withered up her soul, and shut her sympathies within very narrow limits. Her own flesh and blood—Jeff and the doctor, Nurse Haywood and Uncle George— were now all the world held that was dear to her; and even Uncle George was suffering in her opinion as the husband—or rather because he was the slave—of his Julia. Under these circumstances, it was perhaps creditable to poor Jenny that she had been as civil to Mrs. Campden that afternoon as she had been.

Kitty, on the other hand, was actuated by different feelings. Her mother's death had left her—until her father's return, of which, however, she at least still entertained a hope—head of the family; and her soul was filled with the sense of that responsibility. The proposition made on behalf of Mr. Holt did not strike her with that force and significance which it had for her sister; she saw in it a kindness, unexpected indeed, but explicable enough on the ground of his friendship for her father. She looked upon the money as a loan, not as a gift; and, though even so it would be unpleasant to accept it, she did not think it consistent with her duty to those left in her charge to refuse such an offer point-blank. She had not yet made herself aware how their slender finances actually stood, and therefore could not measure the necessity of the case; and she was solicitous not to lose a friend for her dear ones, and still more not to make an enemy. That she could be resolute against dictation, when her heart counselled resistance, has been proved by her refusal of Mrs. Campden's generous proposal to take the baby off her hands; but Jenny had left the room before she had displayed this fortitude.

It was, therefore, under some sort of misunderstanding, rather than disagreement, that the two sisters now met in the little sitting-room, having been summoned thither by the squire's arrival.

"My darlings," said he, gently, "this is a sad day for you; but I thought you would not mind seeing Uncle George."

The sight of these delicate girls, so pale and mournful, in their simple black dresses, affected him deeply. He noticed that Kitty wept, while Jenny was quite dry-eyed, and yet that the latter looked the more pained and hopeless of the two; that was probably, thought he, because of her physical ailment, poor thing. He tenderly embraced them both, and then spoke some hopeful words about their father.

"Jeff says that it is by no means thought to be a desperate case with regard to the *Flamborough Head*, even now, and that persons are still found to insure her, though, of course, at a great premium—— Come, come, girls, cheer up; I hope and trust that my old friend may come home to see his darlings yet."

"Not all his darlings—not the best of them," moaned Kitty, wringing her little hands.

"*I* have no hope, Uncle George," said Jenny, quietly.

"Well, well; time will show, lass. My prayer is, that your poor father may be restored to be your guide and protector. But if it please God to deny this, material matters will, on the other hand, be less untoward with you. His life is insured—though, singularly enough, I never knew it—in a Company of which I am a director, for five thousand pounds. The worst is, that some time may elapse before the proof arrives—that is——"

"We understand," interrupted Jenny, quietly. "Mrs. Campden explained it."

"Yes, yes; and about Holt's offer, and so on. Well, I have been thinking since that you might have some hesitation in accepting that. Now, suppose a little arrangement should be entered into between you two and me, no one else knowing anything about it; there would not be the same objection, would there? Here are two hundred pounds—that would be enough, eh?"

"Oh yes, Uncle George; but——"

"Now, my dear Kitty, it's a loan; you need have no false pride in the matter."

" But I am not sure that we shall want it, Uncle George, at least not just at present. We shall live very, very quietly now; shall we not, Jenny, you and I? and as for Tony, he will soon be off our hands. It is such an indescribable pleasure to us to think that the poor boy will for the next year or two, at all events, feel no disadvantage from his change of fortune, since you have so kindly offered to send him to Eton."

"To Eton?" said Mr. Campden, reddening. "Yes; to be sure there was some talk of that. But Mrs. Campden was thinking perhaps some other school—I mean in the boy's own interest —might, under the circumstances, be more suitable."

" Oh dear; I am so sorry!" said Kitty. "Papa went away so pleased that Tony was to go to Eton; and mamma—I think, somehow, dear mamma had set her heart upon it. Moreover, Uncle George, you promised it," observed Kitty gravely.

" Well, my dear, I believe I did, and I should like to do it still; but, the fact is, Mrs. Campden thinks—— However, no matter about that; I promise you the boy shall go to as good a school as Eton."

"Subject to what Mrs. Campden thinks."

"Oh Jenny, Jenny!" cried Kitty reprovingly.

Mr. Campden's face turned from red to white. It was the first time either of the girls had seen Uncle George "put out," except by his wife.

"You should not speak to your father's friend like that, Jenny," said he severely. "It is not becoming in a young girl."

"It is becoming in no one to break his word, and least of all because——"

"Be quiet, Jenny!" cried her sister, with passionate pleading. "How can you, *can* you talk so, when Uncle George has just been so kind!"

"What Jenny says will make no difference as to that," said the squire coldly. "The two hundred pounds are quite at your service."

"But I am not sure that we shall want them, Uncle George," said Kitty timidly, and flushing very much at the sight of Mr. Campden's pocket-book. It held those very same notes which had been offered to John Dalton on the eve of his luckless departure from Riverside, and been declined.

"You will certainly want them, my dear," said he; "if not to-day, to-morrow. It is ridiculous to suppose that you can keep house —and pay unlooked-for expenses also—on your little income, without any hope of its being increased."

"We *have* hope, Mr. Campden," said Jenny slowly. "And I for my part at least, had rather not take——"

"You talk very foolishly, girl," interrupted Mr. Campden with irritation: "if you suppose you can earn your own living, you must be mad. I know you are thinking of your lacework; but Lady Skipton was writing about it only the other day to Mrs. Campden, and assured her that, commercially speaking, it was valueless."

It was a cruel thing to say, even in anger, but the squire little knew what pain he was inflicting. The thought that her little private note to Lady Skipton, with its offer of the lace, had been made the subject of correspondence between her ladyship and Mrs. Campden, was gall and wormwood to her. "That woman" must have known, then, that she had tried to sell her wares in Town, and failed.

"It is not the lace at all, Mr. Campden, which

I have in my mind," said Jenny, speaking very firmly.

"What is it then?"

"It is a secret. I cannot tell *you* what it is even if you promised not to tell."

"Jenny, you are insulting me."

"No; I am but telling the truth; though, if I did insult you, it would be only what your wife did to us to-day, and has been doing every day since we were poor."

"This is very sad," said Mr. Campden, looking at Kitty.

"Yes, it is," continued Jenny passionately; "it is very sad to think that one's friends should be so base. I say these things because I am angry; but Kitty thinks the same, though she does not say them."

"There is some frightful mistake," murmured Mr. Campden helplessly. The alteration in his wife's manner towards her late guests since their misfortune had by no means escaped him; but he had flattered himself that he alone had seen it.

"A mistake!" cried Jenny scornfully. "Yes, it is a mistake, and very frightful too, to insult people because they are poor; to patronise them;

to endeavour to humiliate them by gifts at the expense of others. That, however, is what one must needs expect of some natures—women's natures. But that a man—a *man*—should promise something to an old friend, and then, when that friend has been lost at sea, and his wife is dead, and his children desolate, should break his word, at the instigation of another — that, I say, is base !"

In her indignation and bitterness, Jenny had risen to her feet. If she had been a strong big woman, red of face and loud of tongue, one might have set her down as a virago ; but being pale and wan, and speaking most musically all the while, although her words flowed like a torrent, it was impossible for a man to despise her wrath.

" I cannot stay here to listen to these things," said Mr. Campden, also rising from his seat. " I came here, Heaven knows, without expecting any such scene—I wished to do you nothing but kindness, and I wish it still—Kitty."

" I know it, Uncle George, and Jenny knows it," sobbed poor Kitty ; " only, she was put out by the disappointment about Eton : not on her own account, of course, nor even on Tony's, but because it was mamma's wish that—that—and because to-day of all days——"   .

"Yes, yes; I see," said Mr. Campden, his kindly nature reasserting itself; "it has been very unfortunate.   But don't let us part ill friends."

Kitty's answer was to throw her arms about his neck and cover him with tears and kisses.

"Come, Jenny," said he, "you will shake hands with Uncle George?"

"Oh yes; I will shake hands with you—Mr. Campden; and I thank you for all your kindnesses in old times."

"Well, the old times will come again, my girl, some day; and you will be sorry to have been so bitter with us at Riverside, and I should be sorry too—only I shall have forgotten it."

"No, Mr. Campden; you will not have forgotten it, though it is kind of you to say you will; and the old times will *never* come back; they are dead and gone." The tears came into her large eyes, her voice trembled, her frail limbs gave way beneath her, and she would have fallen, but for Kitty's protecting arm, which in a moment encircled her waist.

"Don't speak, darling; don't worry yourself," whispered Kitty; "Uncle George has not gone away angry: there is no mischief done—at least I hope not. And I don't blame you for what you said—no, not one bit."

Whosoever had deserted them, whomsoever they had lost, these two loving hearts were one, and the stronger for their intertwining.

CHAPTER V.

ALTHOUGH Kitty strove to comfort her sister all she could, she was herself filled, not indeed with sorrow for Jenny's plain speaking, for that had her secret approbation, but with apprehensions for the result of it. She felt that there was now a gulf between their late friends at Riverside and themselves, which it would require all her address to bridge over: and they were in such sore need of friends. And Jenny on her part was consumed with regret that she had distressed her sister. As to Mrs. Campden and Mary, she had washed her hands of them for good and all; and even with respect to Uncle George—she could never think of him as Uncle George again; he had shown himself weak beyond expression: whatever she had said (I am afraid she did not quite remember what she *had*

said) fell short of his deserts, and she did not repent
it; but she regretted having selfishly given way to
her own impulses. She felt that others might be
made to suffer for her audacity, who, unlike herself, would have preferred to be patronised, and
humiliated, and laid under obligations, rather than
starve. What right had she to indulge her passionate indignation at the expense of her sister, and
poor Tony, and the unconscious babe? These bitter
reflections occurred to her, as she lay upon her couch
in the drawing-room, racked with pain, and trembling with the excitement of her late interview.
Kitty had been summoned to the baby, and there
was no one to interrupt her solitary thoughts. She
had not wept since she had seen her mother laid in
her grave that morning; the fountain of her tears
was dry, and where it should have been, there was a
fire that seemed to burn up her very brain.

Where was justice—for it was idle to talk of
mercy—where was barest justice fled? What had
they all done to deserve so hard a fate? Could
not the merits of that late departed one win for
her beloved children a spark even of hope? (She
had talked of hope to Mr. Campden, in a momentary spirit of pride, but she had, in fact, next to
none.) Was there no such a thing as genuine

friendship in the world? friendship that would stand the test of——"

"Jenny!"

"My dear Jeff, how you frightened me!" cried she, holding out both hands. "I thought you had gone home with the doctor."

"What! without having had one word alone with you and Kitty? No; I only waited till my betters had had their say."

"You mean Mr. Campden?"

"Yes, of course. But why speak of him in such a tone."

"Oh, it's a long story. I have been a little angry with him because he is rich and we are poor; that's all."

"Well, but that was very wrong. *I* am going to be rich, some day."

"'Some day,' my poor Jeff!"

"Now, don't call me 'poor,' whatever you call me," returned he, smiling; "people in the City don't like it. I was really in earnest, when I said 'some day;' and I mean some early date, *proximo* (you have no idea how classical we are in our business letters). I have not told a soul save yourself, but I should not be the least surprised if Holt was to make me his partner."

" What for ? "

" Well, that is scarcely complimentary, Jenny. How do you know that I have not exhibited a great commercial genius ? Seriously, however, it is because he finds I am an honest man—quite a *lusus naturæ*, I assure you, in his particular line."

" But you are not a man at all, Jeff; though I must say. you look very like one. How you are grown and filled out ! You have got to be quite good-looking ! and how becomiugly you blush."

" Yes ; that is why I am so valuable to Mr. Holt. If one cannot blush oneself, it is something to have a confidential clerk who blushes. Of course I was joking about a partnership, at least for the present ; but there is no calling in which a man can become rich early so easily as in ours. And upon my word I've hopes."

" Ah, dear Jeff, how I envy you !" sighed Jenny. " How I wish I could see any prospect of making a little money !"

" Well, well, don't despair. Of course that depression in the lace-market—the unexpected alteration in the quotations—was very disappointing."

" It was worse than that, Jeff. Can you imagine anything so base as that woman's telling Mrs. Campden of my application, although I had put

'Private and confidential' upon my little note to her ? "

" I can very easily imagine it, my dear Jenny. I have witnessed too many delicate 'operations'— though not in lace—to be astonished at anybody's baseness. However, you have another string to your bow, remember."

" Oh Jeff, have you any good news of that ?"

" Not at present; but then there is no bad news."

" Good. I have been schooled to be thankful for small mercies. I shall ask no more questions. Here is Kitty; perhaps you would like a word with her alone ;" and Jenny was off in a moment. Kitty entered the room with a roll of flannel in her arms, which was the baby.

" My dear Jeff, I can't shake hands, you see. Oh, you naughty boy ! " For the young gentleman, since he could not shake hands, had saluted her with his lips.

" I thought that was what you *meant*, Kitty," said he, with simplicity.

" You thought nothing of the kind, sir ; and I am very angry with you ; or at least I should be, if I had the heart for it. How nice it was of you, dear Jeff, to come so far for a single day, just to——"

"Don't talk like that, Kitty: your dear mother was the kindest friend I ever had or ever shall have; and your poor father——"

"Oh Jeff, do not speak of him as though all hope was gone!"

"I did not intend to do so, Kitty; I only meant that he was to be pitied, as indeed he is."

"Ah, if he only knew! I scarcely venture to wish him to be alive, when I think, that if he is not, dear mamma and he may be even now together. I know not what to hope, nor even to pray, Jeff. Things are very, very bad with us; and yet we are told that they will be so much worse."

"Who says that?" said Jeff, with a flash of his black eyes. "He was a brute, whoever he was."

"Well, it was a lady, my dear Jeff."

"Let us say a woman, Kitty. I can guess who the person was. She told you that it was her duty to speak the whole truth, did she not? We have people in the City who tell us the same, and who are not believed by anybody. If your father is dead, then of course things are bad indeed; but even so, there is some one else, to whose care he confided you when he went away; a friend who will never desert you while life is in him."

"Alas, he has already deserted us, Jeff; or rather, I am afraid we have seriously offended him."

"I think you must be mistaken there, Kitty."

"No, Jeff; it happened this very day. You must not speak of it, because it would hurt Jenny. But I feel we can no longer count upon Uncle George— that was." And Kitty stooped down over her unconscious burden, to hide her tears.

"But I don't mean Uncle George at all," answered the other gravely. "It was to another person that your father spoke these words when he left River-side: 'Remember, you are their only protector now.' Yes, it was to me, Geoffrey Derwent. I was a boy then, but those words made a man of me. They are engraven on my heart; so that no change nor time can ever erase them."

"Oh Jeff, dear Jeff, did he say that?"

"Yes, darling; and more than that (though I did not mean to tell you it for a long, long time; till I should be in a better position to—to speak of such things)—when he was going away—perhaps for ever—and my heart was full for his sake, I thought it would be wrong to—to keep it a secret from him; and I told it, Kitty."

She was sitting on the sofa, with her head bent over the child, so that he could not see her face, and that gave him courage; though his voice trembled, and its tone was hoarse and low.

" I told him how I loved you, Kitty; and—though I was but a boy, friendless and almost penniless— your father (God bless him for it !) was tender and gentle with me, seeing perhaps that I was speaking truth at all events. He promised nothing indeed : how could he ? But he did not deny me. He said, when he came back, we two should speak to- gether about that matter. That was not much, you may say ; but to me it was a great deal—for, Kitty, you are all in all to me. Don't answer me yet ; don't treat me less kindly than your father did ; only promise that some day—years to come, if it must be so—that *we* two may speak together about that matter. But if you have—other views "— here the boy stopped, half-choked—" then tell me now, at once. I shall never blame you ; I shall hope for your happiness with—with the man I am thinking of—in spite of hope."

She shook her head. " You are cruel, like the rest," she murmured.

" *I* cruel ! and to you, Kitty ?" sighed he. " Oh no. Whatever seems good to you and right to you, will be sufficient for me. If you say 'No'— just 'No' to the question that my heart is asking,

I will ask no other. You shall never be troubled by me this way again. The purpose of my life as respects you and yours will be just the same. I shall still do all that in me lies for you, for Jenny, for Tony, for that poor little one who lies in your arms. I shall be always their Protector, if not their only one."

"What is it you want me to say, Jeff?" said Kitty suddenly. Her tears were no longer falling: she looked up at him without flinching, though her white face showed her pain.

"Can you ask me, Kitty? It is the simplest of all questions: Do you love me?"

"We all love you, Jeff."

The boy made an impatient gesture. "You are fencing with me, Kitty. Yes or no?"

"I am not fencing, Jeff. I will frankly tell you, that if I were my own mistress, without others depending upon my choice—others whose interests I am bound to consult before my own inclination —I might be foolish enough to say: 'Boy as you are, I will trust your love, and some day entrust my happiness to your keeping.' It would, per-haps, be folly in me, and certainly an injustice to yourself, to say as much; but you are so dear to me, Jeff, that I might have been tempted to do it.

As matters stand, however, it is wholly out of the question. I might well say that on a day like this—the darkest in our lives, with the rustle of the earth upon our mother's coffin-lid still ringing in my ears—your topic is ill chosen; but I am willing to believe that your very love for my dead mother in a manner sanctifies your love for me, and excuses the expression of it. Let me say rather, that neither to-day, nor for many days— nor perhaps for many years to come—is it likely that marriage will be in my thoughts at all. They will be occupied, dear Jeff, with very sober, very simple, and what most folks would call, with very 'uninteresting' things—the making both ends meet in a very humble household; the feeding, and clothing, and teaching them. If they ever get pudding, it will be either Jenny or I who will have to cook it. I shall not probably have the time or the opportunity even to read about love in a novel, much more to make it. That is the programme of my future life, Jeff. It is not pleasant—it is no use pretending that it is—but I mean to make the best of it. Pray, don't make it harder for me by saying any more."

"I will not say a word more now, Kitty——"

"That's right," interrupted she quickly. "It is

close upon the doctor's dinner-hour, and you must not keep him waiting. I hope you will dine with us the next time you come, and pass your opinion on our pudding. We shall be always—always glad to see you, Jeff."

The baby was in her lap now, and she held out her hand for him to shake. Instead of doing so, he carried it slowly to his lips and kissed it.

"God bless you, Kitty!" he said.

"God bless you, Jeff!"

He looked so handsome, so honest, and so loving, that there was a struggle even in that self-sacrificing bosom to add something more; but she did not. She heard him run downstairs, and Jenny call out "Jeff!" as he passed, in vain, and Tony cry, "Jeff! Jeff! where are you going?" without reply; then the front door was opened and closed very quickly, but gently too, as though he who went forth had not, even in his haste, forgotten it was the house of sorrow.

Kitty moved to the window, but too late, because of her little burden; there was nothing to be seen save the thickening dusk and the slow-falling rain. He had gone.

When Jenny entered the room half an hour afterwards—she had been talking tenderly and gravely to Tony in her own chamber—she found Kitty at her mother's desk. It had not been opened since her death, but now the neat little account-books and the memoranda of their scanty in-comings, were all spread out upon the table, with already a note or two of Kitty's own. Jenny took in the situation at a glance.

"Kitty!" cried she, with a burst of penitence, "I have been very wrong. It is you who have the responsibility, and the trouble, and the care of us; while I have only indulged my passion and my pride. If it is not too late—if the mischief I have done is not irreparable—pray, think no more of my opinion, of my prejudices."

"Hush, hush, my darling! You have done no harm, or at least nothing wrong, which is the greater matter."

"You are an angel—you are like our mother," answered Jenny, vehemently; "and I am unworthy to be your sister. Henceforward, I will never oppose what you think right. How is it with us, Kitty? Are we very, very poor? Will it be necessary—shall you ask Mr. Campden for that money?"

"For some of it, darling, I am afraid we must."

"And Mr. Holt? We need not take that—that

loan he offers, need we, Kitty? at least, not yet—
there may be brighter days."

"No, dear; we will not take Mr. Holt's money.
No, no, no!"

There was a calmness and decision in Kitty's
tone which were rare with her; her face was very
pale, and wore a set expression which was new to it.

Jenny looked at her sister for a moment with
wondering eyes, then rushed into her arms.

"Oh, Kitty, I am so glad, so glad!" she cried,
bursting into tears. "Dear Jeff will be dearer to
me now than ever."

"Be silent, Jenny, don't speak of him; I can't
bear it," was the unexpected reply, delivered with
strange vehemence. Then, in gentler but firm
tones she added: "Forgive me, darling, but you
have given me pain. You are wrong, quite wrong,
in thinking—what you said. Here are the bills
and the banker's book; let us look over the
accounts together."

CHAPTER VI.

KITTY'S DREAM.

THAT cynical phrase about "not being able to afford to keep a conscience," has a solid foundation in fact. There are some, indeed, who would rather perish than do anything contrary to their sense of what is right (though even that is a sacrifice which varies with the value men set on individual existence); there are as many more who would perish rather than endure a humiliation—who would take poison rather than swallow their pride. It is only the popular religion—a very different thing from Christianity—that has made Death so terrible as to be weighed against shame; but when it comes to the pinch, Necessity, or what we choose to consider such, overrules the law of the mind. This is a matter upon which drawing-room philosophers and comfortable divines are no judges. It seems so easy—and *is* so easy—to be independent, chaste, and honest, when there is only a temptation to be otherwise; but when the temptation becomes an alternative—on the one side, poverty, death, ruin, for example; on the other hand, competence, not only for ourselves, but for those we love, that is quite another matter. Conscience has then a new antagonist, the first of his own laws; a sense of right, almost as strong as himself, which, allying itself with these various opponents, generally succeeds in overthrowing him. That "second thoughts are best," among all lying proverbs, holds the pre-eminence; second thoughts in morals are never best, but only, as it is natural they should be, second-best.

John Dalton had so left his affairs, that, if he should now be dead and drowned, as it was almost certain he was, he had paid up his legal liabilities, as he imagined, to the last shilling. Even the scoundrels who had "floated" the *Lara* mine could never point to his children as the offspring of a defaulter. His shares would have been paid up in full to the last penny. But his efforts to effect this had left him impoverished indeed: all that his family had to live upon was the interest of some two or three thousand pounds, and a certain small sum which he had left for emergencies in his wife's hands. Moreover, he had unhappily omitted to reckon a few outstanding debts, such as always attend a rich man's expenditure, almost unknown to himself, and which he generally settles with a sudden cheque, and a malediction upon his own forgetfulness. The creditors were of that agreeable kind—may I instance one's tobacconist?—who do not plague us quarterly, nor even half-yearly, for one's little account; but who, when we start upon a sudden for Brazil, and are likely not to come back again, get naturally nervous, and would like to see the colour of our money. When I said that Mrs. Dalton's correspondence had much fallen off in number since the family misfortunes, I should have made honourable exception of these gentlemen, who had not failed to send in their bills to her with the remark that "an early settlement would oblige." Of course, she had acceded to these requests—which, indeed, were only reasonable—but in so doing had not left enough money behind her to defray her own funeral expenses.

This was the conclusion that Kitty was compelled to arrive at, after a careful study of the financial position of the family. Jenny did her best to assist her in the investigation; but she was not so good at figures, and chiefly confined herself to "approving" what her sister made of them, like any City director, except that she did not get five hundred a year for doing it. They had enough, they reckoned, to go on with in their humble fashion—especially as Lucy was leaving them—but, for the present, ready money was indispensable. Under these circumstances, there was nothing for it (even Jenny owned) but to apply to Mr. Campden for some portion of that loan which he had voluntarily placed at their disposal, and which Kitty at least had certainly not unconditionally declined. She therefore despatched a letter to the squire, very warmly and gratefully worded, but at the same time expressing herself as practically as she could with respect to the money itself. If her father should return to them, he would, of course, himself become responsible for the repayment of the loan; and if God had willed it otherwise, the insurance he had effected on his life would enable his children to repay it. A few days ago she would certainly not have used so business-like a style in addressing her correspondent; but now — though without having adopted poor Jenny's views—she was less inclined to wear her heart upon her sleeve, even to Uncle

George. By return of post a letter came from
Riverside in Mrs. Campden's handwriting.

Kitty looked at the envelope with vague alarm.
She had not put "Private" outside her note to the
squire, though she had felt herself inclined to do
so; and was it possible that her late hostess had
opened it, and replied to it herself? She felt a
flush rise to her cheek, for whatever had been her
need, she would never have applied for aid to
Mrs. Campden, nor even to her husband, had she
thought he would have made his wife a confidante
of the fact. He had given Kitty distinctly to understand that the transaction would be a private
one. The envelope was weighty, and contained,
along with a pretty long communication, two five-
pound notes. She had asked the squire for fifty.

"DEAR KITTY," the letter began—"In the absence of Mr. Campden, who is in London, I took
the liberty to open your note, thinking that it
might require an immediate reply. Its contents
have astonished me exceedingly. I am grieved not
only upon your own account, but upon hers of whom
you speak—for whose sake, as you would have me
believe, you have thought proper to make your
very singular application. I cannot think any-

thing would have distressed your poor mother herself more than the step you have thus thought
proper to take. Let us hope, in the sphere to which
she has been removed by an all-wise Providence,
that she is ignorant of the circumstance. What
you have asked Mr. Campden is, in plain English,
to *give* you fifty pounds. There is even an allusion to a larger sum, which it seems you have
been trying to persuade him to promise you, or
which he has promised you of his own head. To
take advantage of my husband in such a matter
is, as you must be well aware, Kitty, to take
advantage of a child; and it is my duty to protect
him against any such attempts. However, I will
confine myself to the fifty pounds. You speak
hopefully, and I hope you have reason for your
confidence, of your poor father's return home; but
if he does return, have you painted to yourself
what will be his true position? Have you—has
anybody—the least cause to suppose that he will
be in a condition to repay the debts of his family?
One of his best friends—and *your* best friend, if
you would permit him to be so—has assured me
that he has gone to Brazil in pursuit of a mere
chimera; that he will come back poorer, if that be
possible, than he went.

"Now, Kitty, it is my bounden duty to speak plainly to you. It is this very carelessness of other people's money that has brought your father to this pass. He gambled away first his own fortune, and then your mother's; and now he seems to expect to use the money of his friends as though it was his own. I have good reasons for stating that he proposed to draw upon my poor husband —while abroad—as on his own banker! You are doubtless shocked at this revelation; yet, if you examine the matter, the difference between your present application and that most outrageous one is only in degree. Fifty pounds, a hundred pounds, two hundred pounds—so we go on when this terrible course has been once begun. You think, perhaps, my husband is made of money, and that it does not signify how much you ask. The money, my dear girl, is nothing indeed compared with the sacrifice of principle that would be involved if it were given you, and to which I, therefore, for one, would never consent. But even the money is something. Mr. Campden is no doubt what some people would call a rich man; but rich people have calls of which poor people have no conception: he has his position in the county to keep up—an imperative duty—and a thousand other

sources of expense, which you would hardly understand should I enumerate them. With respect to
the expenses of the funeral, I have made inquiries,
and considering the simplicity with which it was
conducted, in accordance with your mother's wish
—and which does honour to her good sense—I
find ten pounds will be *ample*, and I therefore
enclose that sum. I am very glad to find that by
frugality and care you will for the future be able
to make both ends meet; always live within your
income, dear Kitty, and then, whatever it may be,
you may account yourself rich.

" I am sorry you did not accept my proposition
with respect to the baby; a home, however, will
always await it at the lodge, should you alter what
I must venture to call your ill-judged resolution.

" And this brings me, Kitty, to another subject,
the importance of which must be my excuse for
once more breaking it to you. Do you know what
you are doing, and do you know whom you are
*un*doing, in rejecting the advances of Mr. Holt?
From him a loan of fifty pounds, or of five hundred,
could indeed be accepted with a good grace, and
would be advanced with something more than
alacrity. If ever there was an example of a girl's
' sinning her chances,' you, Kitty, are surely now

affording it. What excuse you can possibly make
to yourself for rejecting what I may almost call
this gift of Providence, I cannot imagine. You
may have your reasons; but they are most certainly mere personal ones, and you must forgive
me for adding, selfish ones. Do you reflect that it
only rests with you to give to your little household
a natural protector? (At present I do not see how
it is possible for you to leave home even to go out
as a governess.) Some men—nay, most men—
would hesitate to marry a penniless girl surrounded
by incumbrances; but this man is one in a thousand; and yet you treat him as if there was
another such to be picked up any day and any-
where—in Sanbeck, for example. However, I
have said my say.

"Mary sends you her best love; she is making
up a little parcel of things which I hope will prove
useful to you: a dress or two that she has out-
grown, but which we think will just suit your
figure; and when the spring comes on, she will
doubtless find other articles that you may make
available. Always your sincere friend and well-
wisher,

"JULIA CAMPDEN.

"P.S.—I think it will be better that you should

treat this note as private and confidential. Pray, consult *your own* good sense before replying to the contents of it. Jenny has doubtless many good points, but the state of her health must alone prevent her exercising a dispassionate judgment."

This letter was a terrible blow. There was nothing in it to give ground for absolute quarrel; but Kitty felt that it henceforth divided her and hers from the Riverside people, as by a great gulf. She even believed that it had been written with that express object; in which she probably did the writer wrong. A more acute woman than Mrs. Campden might, indeed, have expected to arouse some angry rejoinder, which would have given her a good excuse for breaking with her needy kinsfolk altogether; but the mistress of Riverside saw nothing offensive in the letter she had composed. She meant to put her foot down with respect to any further attempt upon her husband's purse; and she used the opportunity, without scruple, of placing Kitty's hopeless position before her, and of pointing out the one way of escape; but she had no intention of deliberate insult. She had, nevertheless, the sagacity to understand that Jenny would view her letter as such, and hence she marked it "private and confidential." Though she had not hesitated to break the seal of a communication addressed to another, she gave her correspondent credit for more delicate scruples—and took advantage of them. The children of this world are not only wiser than the children of light, but they trade upon their simplicity. A rogue will often deny the existence of an honest man, to save his own credit, though well aware that he is lying; but when he has found one he will use his honesty for his own purposes.

Kitty, too, was well aware that Jenny would have at once designated the writer of such a communication as dishonourable, mean, cruel, and a number of other perhaps not wholly inapplicable adjectives. The gift of the cast-off raiment would have been especially offensive to her. Whereas Kitty, in her humility, and her consideration for those committed to her trust, was resolved not to take offence, even if it had been purposely offered to her. It was unnecessary upon Mrs. Campden's part to have been so energetic against any future application to her husband. Nothing, *nothing* would have henceforth induced her to ask help of Uncle George. If the worst came to the worst, she would rather sell herself, as this woman was urging

her to do, to Richard Holt. It would be horrible,
it would be shameful; but the humiliation could
not be deeper, and the advantage to others would
be great and certain. If those two five-pound
notes had been the wages of shame, she could
hardly have regarded them with a more intense
loathing. Her fingers closed upon them fiercely,
savagely; she longed to tear them to pieces; most
of all, she craved to return them, with a few civil
but cutting words. That money, she felt, was as
much given to her out of charity—and that a
charity which had no love in it—as the cast-off
clothes which were to follow. She felt like a beggar
(though she had never been one) who has been
refused the alms he asked, and has had a crust of
bread flung at him instead. If she could only have
done without the crust, and have flung it back to the
giver! There was one way which would, she knew,
have Jenny's hearty concurrence, namely, that they
should sell some article of furniture in Bleabarrow,
and pay the undertaker's bill with the proceeds.
But Kitty, always just, reflected that such a course
would excite country gossip, and bring great dis-
credit upon the squire, who was not answerable for
his wife's actions, and indeed hardly for his own.
Another alternative was to borrow the money of

Dr. Curzon. But they surely had had enough of borrowing—or rather of the attempt to borrow; and, moreover, they already owed the doctor for many a professional visit. No; Kitty felt she must take these two five-pound notes, and acknowledge their receipt with words of thanks.

She had retired to her own room to read the letter, directly she had recognised Mrs. Campden's handwriting, and now she meant to destroy it, before she saw Jenny; so that she could honestly say "I have it not," if her sister asked to read it. But hearing Jenny's knock at the door, she thrust the letter with its enclosure into her pocket, and rose to meet her.

"Well, Kitty, what news? I need scarcely ask, however; I can read it reflected in your flushed face. From a reason over which he has no control —if you can call his wife 'a reason'—Mr. Campden cannot keep his promise."

"My dear Jenny, you said you wouldn't——"

"I said I wouldn't interfere with what you resolved upon. I may surely flatter my own foresight by 'spotting,' as Jeff calls it, these good people beforehand. The squire is weak as water: he would if he could, he says, but he can't."

"He says nothing of the kind, Jenny. The

letter does not come from him at all, but from Mrs. Campden. She opened my note, it seems, in his absence."

Jenny smiled. "What luck she must have thought it! I can imagine her gloating over a letter meant for somebody else."

"Oh Jenny!" cried Kitty, reprovingly. The thought crossed her mind: "What a strange bitterness possesses my dear sister! Three months ago—nay, ten days since, while our mother was yet alive—such sentiments would never have found harbour within her, far less expression."

"Well," continued Jenny, "of course she will not let her husband lend us the money, 'as a matter of principle.'"

"It is something like that," said Kitty, reluctantly. "She has sent us, however, ten pounds, which will, I hope, be sufficient."

"I am glad it was no more," said Jenny, "for two reasons: first, because it corroborates my view of her; secondly—— But never mind 'secondly' for the present. Well, what else did she say, besides how fond she was of us, and how it was all for our own good? May I see the letter?"

"It is marked private and confidential."

"That was foolish of her, because I now know

what it was about. You do not wish, I suppose,
dear, to talk upon the subject?"

"No, Jenny; because it would be of no
use."

"But you have not made up your mind?" cried
Jenny, eagerly. "Before you do that, I must
speak to you, darling; I must, I must!"

"No, dear; I have made up my mind to nothing
—except that we must take these ten pounds."

"Was there no message from Mary—dear Mary,
who used to hang about your neck so lovingly but
a few weeks ago?"

"Well, no; nothing particular. She is going
to send us some things that her mother thinks may
be useful to us."

"*What* things?" cried Jenny, contemptuously.
"A pot of marmalade; some shilling novels; a
yard of flannel—such as they send to the hospitals."

"There may be some flannel," said Kitty,
quietly.

"Oh, I see: old clothes that are too fine for the
lady's maid. We are in the first stage of our
descent, my dear; they will send us next year old
clothes that are not fine enough for her. For my
part, I always thought Mary a humbug."

"Don't say that, Jenny; she is not strong, that

is all. You might just as well say half the world
are humbugs."

"Half the world! I say nine hundred and
ninety-nine hundredths of them are so! What
saith the Scripture: 'One man out of a thousand
have I known'—There is Jeff, for example, and
there is the doctor—" but 'one woman in a thousand
I have not known.' Or, at all events, she is not
Mary Campden."

To this outburst, Kitty replied nothing; and
further questioning upon Jenny's part was put a
stop to by the entrance of Tony in a wild state of
excitement. Something had come for him " regis-
tered" by the post; he had met the postman in
the village, and gone back to the office to sign for
it; and what did they think it was! They would
never guess if they guessed for ever: it was a
watch and chain; a beautiful gold watch and
chain!

"Why, Tony, who could have sent it?" cried
Jenny, delighted at the lad's delight; then the joy
faded out of her face, and she looked at Kitty,
whose cheeks had become crimson.

"Well, I don't know," cried Tony. "I should
have thought it was Jeff, only dear old Jeff could
never have—— The post-mark was Cornhill, too,

and he said Mr. Holt's office was close by Cornhill."

"It came from Mr. Holt," said Jenny; "I know his handwriting. We must send it back again."

"Send it back?" cried Tony, growing very red in his turn. "Why should I send it back? I think it was very kind of him. He has always been very civil to me; and every fellow has a watch who goes to Eton."

"I don't think we can send it back, Jenny," said Kitty, gravely. "It is sent to Tony, you see."

"Yes; that is so mean of him," answered Jenny, stamping her little foot. "He knew there would be a difficulty about returning it."

"It would be exceedingly rude to return it, just because you don't like him," said Tony, confidently. "If you did, you may depend on it, he would never send me anything again. See here; when you touch this button, the back opens, and there are the wheels and things. My dear Kitty, what *are* you at? Jenny, Kitty is crying into my watch-works."

And indeed, while endeavouring to be interested in Tony's treasure, poor Kitty had not been able to restrain a tear. She laughed the matter off, however, in an hysterical sort of way, and before the afternoon post went, had helped Tony with his letter of thanks to the sender: his tutor and literary adviser in ordinary, Jenny, having flatly refused to have anything to do with it.

It gave Kitty a pang, we may be sure; but since the present was to be accepted, it was needful that it should be duly acknowledged. That watch and its works cost her more than it cost the buyer; it haunted her thoughts all that day, and even her dreams at night. This is what she dreamed: She was in a room full of figures like those at Madame Tussaud's, except that they all moved by machinery. There was her dead mother looking at her with pitying eyes; and her lost father, with changed, remorseful face, his hair and clothes all wet. These and many others revolved slowly round her at some distance, but none approached her. She herself was borne slowly but irresistibly forward towards a figure with outstretched arms. It was Richard Holt. His chest was bare, and where his heart should have been, she saw toothed wheels at work, all gold; just as she had seen in Tony's watch, only larger. She heard them moving and clicking with a harsh monotonous noise, louder and louder as she drew nigh. Then as she came quite close, the arms—a picture she had seen in a

" History of the Inquisition " at home no doubt suggested this—suddenly shot out knives and daggers, and were just about to enfold her, when with a shrill scream she woke.

CHAPTER VII.

AN AUTHOR AND HIS EDITOR.

ABOUT halfway between the Bank of England and
Basinghall Street*— a position somewhat typical
of many of its tenants—lies Abdell Lane. A street
so narrow, although the houses are but three-
storied, that in the sunniest days it is always dim
and cool, except at noontide; while throughout the
winter and half the spring, the inhabitants pursue
their avocations solely by artificial light. Their
callings are various; and in many cases would be
difficult to explain to the public satisfaction; and
yet they have some right to be called respectable,
since a rent of about two hundred pounds *per annum*
is paid *per room*. Off Abdell Lane lies Abdell Court,
connected with the larger thoroughfare by a huge
arch (itself honeycombed by human tenements),
through which the astonished passenger comes

---

* In this street is situated the Court of Bankruptcy.

upon a tree, a pump, and a paved yard, in which
for hours at certain seasons the sun is distinctly
visible. The rents are higher here than in the
lane, although the place is only approachable by
foot-passengers. In fact, that is a circumstance
which is a ground of boast to its residents, since it
shows that the commercial element (in the shop
form) does not intrude itself. On the side of each
door are painted in black and white the names of
each occupant, as in Lincoln's Inn and the Temple;
but there are no lawyers in Abdell Court. They
are chiefly brokers, with a good sprinkling of that
mysterious class of gentry called " financial agents."
Unpromising as the material soil appeared, the seed
of many a goodly mercantile tree had been dropped
in Abdell Court, to grow and grow, and to bear
golden fruit; also other trees, quite as promising,
but which, never coming to maturity, are by many
contumeliously termed "plants." On the ground-
floor of one of these houses there sits, in what
might be called by contrast with its congeners, quite
a spacious apartment, a gentleman with whom we
have made acquaintance under other circumstances.
Black and gray are now his only wear, but the
neatness and completeness of Mr. Holt's attire is
almost as remarkable as it was at Riverside. Per-

haps it is the effect of that sombre dress, but he certainly looks paler and older than when we saw him last : the hair about his temples has thinned, and the lines about his mouth have deepened; if we did not know that his investments are always made with sagacity, and have never given him cause to lose a wink of sleep, we should call his expression careworn. He has an open ledger before him, and a pen in his hand; yet he is not engaged in calculation. A letter, in a large, round, and rather sprawling hand, lies on the page beneath his eyes, and he is conning it attentively.

" Dear Mr. Holt," it runs—" I cannot say how much I am obliged to you for your beautiful present; the watch is much too handsome, I am afraid, for a boy like me, but I will try to take great care of it. I have just found out that it strikes the hours and the quarters. We have been in great trouble, as Jeff will have doubtless told you ; but my sisters are pretty well in health, and beg to be remembered to you.—I am yours truly and obliged,

                              " Anthony Dalton.

" P.S.—Please give my love to Jeff."

Mr. Holt had read this somewhat bald epistle half-a-dozen times, and yet was as interested in it as ever. " It is cleverly written," he muttered to himself; " but it is not all one piece. ' Much too handsome,' and ' Will try to take great care ' — that is not the boy's. I wonder which of the girls helped him with it? ' Jeff will have told you ; ' that is like Jenny's touch. She pretends to believe that I only hear of their welfare through Derwent ; and then, again, ' Give my love to Jeff,' sounds like her sharp tongue. She writes that to annoy me. But then she would never have made him say that they begged to be remembered to me. I am sure that's Kitty ; dear, delicious, tender-hearted Kitty ! " he heaved a deep sigh, and stroked his forehead with his hands.

" How nearly I lost her ! " he went on softly to himself. " If things had not gone just as they have, she would be by this time out of my reach. What a frightful risk did that madman make me run ! " He rose from his seat, and pulling down the window, although the day was bitterly cold, stood facing the draught. " Two months, three months, four months, and not a scrap of news of the ship. All must surely be safe now. The very stars in their courses have fought for me. However, it is the

very last boon that I will ever ask of Fortune;
hereafter, I am independent of her. If I were
bankrupt to-morrow my books would be a model.
There is not a flaw from first to last. If it
had happened otherwise, I wonder if I could have
weathered the storm? With the world, perhaps;
but with him never. He would have been implac-
able, unmerciful. It would have been no wonder,
poor devil. And *she*—yes, she would have loathed
me. I can understand now how it is that men who
cannot possess those they love, are driven to kill
them; as to killing themselves, that is the most
natural thing in the world; and next to that—yes,
I can understand it."

Besides the usual almanac in its frame, and one
or two plans of estates in the West Indies and elsewhere, there were several huge maps hung up in
the room, to one of which he now directed his
attention. This was a map of South America,
showing a great deal of the ocean that lies between
us and it, with the track of steamers marked out
upon it. He had done so many a time before, and
he now again took his pen, and with the handle of
it traced out the course. So engaged was he in this
occupation, that he did not notice a knock at his
door, nor the entrance of a visitor, until his voice—

a rich, unctuous, and somewhat boastful voice—announced his presence.

"Hollo, Holt; how are you? Studying a sea-chart, eh? That looks dangerous for somebody, since you are a shipowner."

"Yes," answered the other, coolly; "I was trying to fix upon the most convenient spot for scuttling a craft."

"Well, begad! you looked as if you really *were* when you first caught sight of *me*. South America, eh? Brazil, I suppose? Mines, for a hundred!"

"You are always right as a rule, Dawkins; and since this particular case happens to be the exception, that proves it. My mind was not fixed on the land at all, but on the sea. I was wondering whether, by any possibility, the *Flamborough Head*, could be still above water."

"I'll bet you ten to one against it; come, I'll bet you twenty. You have not underwritten her, have you?"

"Not I. I was not thinking of the vessel at all but of a poor fellow who sailed in her, John Dalton."

"Oh, indeed. Friend of yours, I remember. Well, I shall say nothing against him, then. But

of all the overbearing, insolent fellows I ever met—
without a penny to bless himself, too—he was
about the worst. By jingo! you should have heard
what he said to Lady Beevor, in my own house,
under my own roof. We all thought he was off
his head."

"Yet he was a general favourite, and thought
very agreeable," observed Holt.

"Agreeable? Then I don't know what it is to
be agreeable."

"Possibly," said the other, dryly; "or perhaps
you annoyed him. If Dalton was rubbed the wrong
way, you saw sparks."

"Sparks, begad! It was a general conflagration.
Lady Beevor has never forgiven my asking him
to meet her. It would have been a liberty in
Rothschild; but for a ruined man! For it was
after he *was* ruined, in that *Lara* mine. Curiously
enough, I came to talk to you about that very thing.
You never had anything in it yourself, I believe?"

"Why do you say that, my good sir, when you
know I *had*?"

"Well, well, don't snap my nose off. It was a
piece of delicacy on my part, because I knew you
plumed yourself on never being connected with
anything shady."

"Oh, I see. Why didn't you say you were going to be delicate? I could scarcely come to that conclusion from analogy."

"I don't know about analogy," said Mr. Dawkins, frankly. "I came here on business. There are people still inquiring about that mine, I hear."

"Indeed? Do you want to buy any shares? They are not quoted, but they can be got cheap— except for the liability they entail."

"Well, no; I don't exactly want to buy any— myself. But, do you know"—here he dropped his voice to a whisper—"Beevor does not think so badly of them."

"So badly of them as *what?*" answered Holt, contemptuously. "If he thought well of them, why didn't he buy some of Dalton's? He had an opportunity, you tell me; and Dalton, poor fellow, would have been only too glad to sell. You know what everybody else knows, I suppose, about the Lara ?"

"Yes ; but there's that fellow Tobbit, the expert——" Mr. Holt made a sign for silence, and touched a hand-bell.

There entered a handsome young fellow from the next apartment, where, indeed, he could have

been seen sitting at his desk, throughout this interview, through the.glass door which communicated
between the two rooms.

"Mr. Derwent, you can take an hour, if you
please; I shall be here myself till three."

"Thank you, sir." The young man was about to
leave the room, when his eye fell on Tony's letter;
the colour came into his face, and he hesitated, as
though about to ask a question.

"I had news of our friends in Sanbeck, by-the-
bye, this morning," observed Holt, carelessly;
"they desired to be remembered to you."

Jeff bowed, and passed into the inner room,
from which another door communicated with the
passage. Not until he was seen from the window
crossing the courtyard did Mr. Dawkins speak
again.

"You have a new clerk, I see, Holt. He has
an honest face; but he is deuced young to be
trusted."

"Yes; but I don't trust him."

"Oh, I see. Some relative, I suppose? Comes
from the country, I think you said?"

"I didn't say so; but he does."

"Do you think he heard me mention Dalton's
name?"

"No; and if he did, it would make no difference. I only sent him out because I had no occasion for his services just now, and I know the lad pines for the open air. His life has been passed in it."

"That is very considerate of you. Where do you think he is gone? to Primrose Hill?"

Some people have no resources in themselves: Mr. Dawkins was not one of these. He could even laugh by himself—at a joke of his own making—and he did it now.

"My dear Holt, what a deep card you are!" said he, admiringly. "It is a wise man who has a fool for his clerk." Then he proceeded to business. It does not concern us to know how these two gentlemen discussed the character of Mr. Tobbit, the great mining expert, or to what conclusion they came; let it suffice to say that Mr. Dawkins departed from Abdell Court convinced, despite the opinion of his millionaire friend, that speculation in *Laras* would be very unprofitable.

Let us rather follow the footsteps of Geoffrey Derwent during his hour's holiday. It was not the first by many that his employer had given him during the wearisome days he had passed in his new calling; he had really shown the consideration to him which Mr. Dawkins had suggested in irony, and had treated him with marked politeness at all times. Moreover, he had given him an insight into business affairs, for which Geoffrey was more grateful than for all else. It gave him hopes of making his own way in the world, when he came of age, and the slender fortune should accrue to him of which Mr. Campden was the trustee. It was even possible, he thought, that the money might be advanced to him by his good-natured guardian before that period. It is amazing how far a good introduction, backed by tolerable wits and a little money, will go in certain City callings which (like the ham in the sandwich) lie between the Commercial and the Professional, and yet belong by rights to neither. Notwithstanding his speech to Mr. Dawkins, Mr. Holt did put trust in Geoffrey, for he had found out that the young fellow could hold his tongue; and, as he never confided to him anything discreditable, it was fair to suppose that the business of Holt and Company, though certainly of a heterogeneous description, was *bonâ fide* and respectable. Indeed, as Jeff reflected, how could it have been otherwise, since Mr. Dalton had been (as he understood) in some measure connected with it? nay, still more, had not Mrs. Dalton herself recommended him to his present employer?

This fact alone had really given Jeff a certain
respect for Mr. Holt, which, as we have seen he,
had been far from entertaining at Riverside; and,
being very sensitive to kindness, this feeling would,
in any other case under the same circumstances,
have grown to be regard ; but it is quite possible
to respect people without liking them—indeed, it
is almost as common as to like them without
respecting them—and Jeff disliked his employer
very cordially. He would work for him faithfully,
and consult his interests as though they were his
own. But he could not return goodwill for what
he felt was only a pretence of it. Every act of
civility of his employer he, in fact, more or less
resented, since he was well aware that he was
indebted for it to Kate Dalton. He knew that
the other calculated upon his telling the truth
concerning his life in Abdell Court, and was
resolved that he should have nothing but good
to tell. He was not even afraid of that pretty
constant correspondence that he must have been
aware went on between his enemy Jenny and his
young assistant. There was security in Jeff's
honesty, equal to any guarantee that could be
got with sign and seal in the neighbourhood of
Abdell Court. Holt had not been sorry that his

one invitation to Jeff to dine with him at his club had been respectfully declined, upon the transparent pretence of a previous engagement; business relations run comparatively easy even when folks are not *en rapport* with one another, but social intercourse is more difficult to be maintained. Mr. Holt had never so much as inquired where Jeff's lodgings were, and Jeff was not likely to volunteer the information: they were two very small rooms, in a suburb of Islington, which had been recommended to him, through Mrs. Dalton, by Mrs. Haywood. They were cheap and clean, and he would be able to see green fields from them when the spring came. In spite of his ardour for work, and for "getting on," which was immense, he pined for the country, even in these winter days. But on the occasion of which we speak—his hour's holiday—he did not go, as was suggested, to Primrose Hill; he bent his steps to a spot which puts forth leaves at every season, Paternoster Row. What would Mr. Dawkins have thought of his friend's sagacity, had he guessed he employed a clerk who was not only a fool, but an author! Yet so it must be, since Jeff enters an establishment over which is written, " Office of ' The Smellfungus Magazine,' " and, passing through the outer apartment, which coarse minds would call a book-shop, knocks at a little door inscribed "Editor's Room." It is that knock which betrays him to us; any would-be contributor might have gone so far as to knock—but not like that. The knock of a would-be contributor, especially one of tender years, is a very modest one; it sounds like that of a poor relation, or of a little child who cannot reach the knocker except with the tips of his fingers. Now, Jeff's summons, given sharply with the knob of his umbrella, was the knock of an accepted contributor, and something more: of a contributor who hasn't been paid.

He did not even wait for the answering "Come in," but entered at once. "The City"—whose motto, like that of poor Dalton's travelling companion, is "Push"—had already done a great deal for Jeff. Besides, he was still in some respects that most audacious and irreverent thing in nature, a boy. We have at present only seen him in the society of ladies, or of his natural guardian, or of his employer; but with the world at large Mr. Geoffrey Derwent was something more than at his ease. When he suspected that anyone was imposing upon him, he was particularly free-spoken, to the verge of rudeness. He had not the modest and retiring manners which good and charitable people are accustomed to attribute to literary geniuses when discovered young.

It must be owned that there was little in the sanctum into which Jeff thus impetuously intruded to excite veneration. It was a little stuffy room, lit by a skylight, and boasting of no other furniture than a bookcase, filled with volumes of "The Smellfungus Magazine," a table, and two chairs; but in one of these two chairs was a Being who ought to have commanded respect, for he was an Editor. A small, plump man, of cheerful aspect, whiskerless and bald, he presented the appearance of one who had been endeavouring to get rid of all his hair for five-and-forty years, and had triumphantly succeeded. He so beamed with blandness and good-nature that it was like being at Brighton, or standing in front of one of Mr. Dyce's pictures, to look at him; you felt you wanted shade.

"How are you, Mr. Derwent? Delighted to see you," said he, holding out a podgy hand, and pressing Jeff's with fervency. "I have just been correcting your proof for next month's number. I never saw so rapid an improvement in so young a writer—it's marvellous."

"Yes; I thought that second one would fetch you, myself," said Jeff coolly.

"Fetch me? Oh, I see! Well, the quaintness of the matter of course goes for something. But as I said to you before, I cannot but think that the mind which could grasp the salient points of so dry a theme—could so clothe dry bones with flesh and blood—might essay something original."

"The mind has done it," observed Jeff dryly, producing a manuscript from his pocket. "Here is a story of old times: local colouring, archæological details, spirit of chivalry; in short, the whole boiling."

"The whole—— Oh, I see! You mean it is all redolent of antiquity. Found in a chest, I hope, as I suggested, with a few words of introduction to explain the circumstance. Good; and stated, I perceive, with great frankness and simplicity. You find it easy to be frank, Mr. Derwent, I daresay?"

"My nature, Mr. Sanders," observed Jeff indifferently.

"Yes. Now what astonishes me in your writing is its objectiveness."

"Ah! that astonishes myself," said Jeff, with a little yawn.

There was a long pause.

"Why, bless my soul," said the editor, whose face was now invisible behind the manuscript, "this is a satire!"

"I should rather think it was," replied Jeff, "and a deucedly good satire too."

"Eh!" Mr. Sanders looked over the top of the manuscript at Jeff. The young gentleman's face was imperturbable; he was tapping his right boot with his umbrella. "This is most extraordinary," murmured the editor.

"That is quite my idea of it," observed the other. "I never wrote anything half so good before."

"I was not referring to the manuscript," rejoined Mr. Sanders, blandly; "that is good, no doubt—in its way. But satires are scarcely quite the sort of thing for 'The Smellfungus Magazine.'"

"I didn't mean it for 'The Smellfungus,'" cried Jeff.

"Eh! what?" The editor looked up again, but Jeff was only tapping his other boot.

"This is not for you. This is to go to some magazine that pays. Pray, don't be angry, my dear sir; I am aware that your magazine is solvent —I mean, that pays its contributors."

"Now, this is hard," said Mr. Sanders, looking at his book-shelves for sympathy; "for it was

I who brought this young man out—correct me,
if I am mistaken, Mr. Derwent, but I think I
was the first—as editor of ' The Smellfungus Magazine '——"

"And proprietor," interrupted Jeff. "That is
where the shoe pinches. The literary side of your
character is perfection; it is the financial side which
is in fault. I have never seen the colour of your
money."

"So young," murmured Mr. Sanders, "and yet
so grasping; this is quite a revelation to me."

"Very good," said Jeff; "I shall make no extra
charge on that account, but I must have twenty
pounds for the story."

"Youth is sanguine," observed Mr. Sanders;
"and likewise full of high spirits. You must be
joking."

But Jeff only looked in the fire, and repeated,
"Twenty pounds."

"Well, I'll tell you *what*," said Mr. Sanders,
clapping his knee, like a man who has resolved
to do something regardless of expense—"I'll *tell
you what*. In consideration of the two papers I
have had for nothing, added to the cost of this
story—for there must be no doubt for the future
about the market value of such articles—I will give

you five pounds. But it must be understood that you give 'The Smellfungus' the refusal of your next work, and at the same proportionate price."

"I'll take the five pounds," said Jeff, after a little pause, " on account. Or, look here: pay me ten pounds down, and you shall have the story."

The deft celerity with which Mr. Sanders produced his cheque-book, filled in a cheque, and also a receipt upon stamped paper, was quite pleasant to see. " Short accounts make long friends," said he cheerfully. " And now, my dear sir, that business is over, let me congratulate you on having permanently joined the staff of 'The Smellfungus.' I see before you a great—or at least a considerable future. You have the art—a very rare one—of making dry details palatable; of putting fire, into old-world facts. All you want are materials. You must come and dwell in the shadow of the British Museum."

" I live at Islington," observed Jeff simply.

" Then you must come by the 'bus to Blooms-bury. The British Museum has been bequeathed to you by the nation to furnish you with facts for ' The Smellfungus Magazine.' "

" Very good," said Jeff. " I will accept the legacy."

"It is wonderful to me how—out at Islington—you can have procured such materials as you have done. However, the whole affair is remarkable: that at your time of life your taste should lead you to grasp these details of the past——"

"So young, so grasping," interrupted Jeff. "Well, I must be off now. Ta-ta."

"Good-bye, my young friend, good-bye," said Mr. Sanders impressively. Then softly repeated to himself: "Ta-ta. He said Ta-ta. That lad is a phenomenon. Antiquarianism is a passion with him, and yet how he talks! I wonder whether Chatterton talked like that? He reminds me very much of Chatterton—in some respects.

CHAPTER VIII.

THE EXODUS.

WHEN an overwhelming grief befalls us, it seems for the moment, even to the humblest, to dwarf all other cares. It is only the rich, however, who can afford to indulge it. With the poor, the next day, or the day after, some miserable need pushes divine Sorrow from her stool, and compels attention. Even Kate Dalton, whose sense of duty was so strong, and whose consciousness of responsibility so keen, had in the anguish of her loss underrated the more sordid troubles that were awaiting her. The cold touch of Death had numbed her somewhat to the meaner pain. But though the weight of sorrow still oppressed her sorely, she now began to feel the other burdens that pressed upon her. Lucy was gone, her wages paid to the last farthing, and her fare to town—but without any present such as her young mistress yearned to make her; and her loss was felt, but not in gain. One mouth the less to feed made but small difference in the household expenses, already reduced to the most economical figure. Do what she could, Kitty found her little income did but just keep pace with her outgoings. And there were still some debts. Dr. Curzon's bill—which must have grown to be a pretty long one by this time—had not yet been sent in; and Kitty dared not ask for it. Yet it seemed to her shocking, and almost sacrilegious, that what was due for medical attendance on her poor mother in those later weeks, as well as on Jenny, should not be settled. The parcel of cast-off raiment had come from Riverside, and Kitty had humbly arrayed herself in one of Mary's dresses. It was nothing more, she had said to herself, than hundreds of well-born and well-bred girls, who are not rich, are wont to do. "You will not be offended if I send you baby's pelisse, who has grown out of all knowledge," is a very usual thing for one mother to write to another who is her friend or relative, but happens not to be so rich in this world's goods. It is as common as Dick's old clothes being "cut up" for his brother Jack. And it is the same, or almost the same, with other garments. Yet somehow Kitty felt it. The change from complete

ɪ 2

equality with her cousin to this state of depend-
ence, obligation, subordination—there was no actual
term for it—had been too sudden for it to be
accepted yet as a matter of course.

Jenny, who had been reading about "doles" in
her old books, used to speak of these gratuitous
garments as "the Riverside dole," and could not be
persuaded to make use of them. Some of the furniture from Cardigan Place had come packed in
sacking; and "When my clothes are worn out,
Margate and I are going to set to work at dress-
making with *that*," she said. "Mrs. Campden will
like to see me in sackcloth, I know; and it will no
doubt be very becoming."

But neither Kitty's meekness nor Jenny's mock-
humility availed them in a financial point of view,
even though the former affected a distaste for
butcher-meat—which was essential for her delicate sister — and took to eating bread and
cheese.

One afternoon Mrs. Campden drove over to the
Nook, and found their little dining-table spread
with one chop for Jenny, and the loaf and cheese.
Tony, as often happened now, had been asked to
dine by the good doctor.

"Cheese is very bad for you, Kitty," said she,

taking in the situation at a glance; "and I am afraid you will find it false economy."

"It agrees with me very well, I thank you," said Kitty, with the nearest approach to bitterness that her gentle nature had ever shown.

"Well, I am glad of that; but I think a good dinner would be an excellent thing for you. If you will come home with me to-day—you and Jenny—I will send you back at night. Mary is away at the Skiptons, in Eaton Square, as you know, but Mr. Campden and I will do our best to make the evening pass agreeably."

"I don't like to leave baby for so many hours, thank you," said Kitty.

"Very well; then I won't ask Jenny to come alone, because I know she hates to be separated from you."

"Quite right," said Jenny; "I do."

It was astonishing, as Mrs. Campden afterwards observed, how soon that girl had lost her manners. Some folks were always independent of mere position in that respect, but Jenny was evidently the creature of circumstances. It was only her being in ill-health that had made people imagine her to have delicate susceptibilities and so forth. Her good-breeding had been in reality but skin-deep.

If Mrs. Campden, however, was severe on Jenny, she was very gracious to Kitty. "Ah, my dear, Mary writes that Eaton Square with Leonora Skipton is not to compare with Cardigan Place and Cousin Kitty. She sticks to old friends, I promise you. I have said my say, you know, about the matter; but you can hardly imagine how Mary clings to the hope of seeing you resume your proper place in the world."

To this Kitty replied nothing; and presently Mrs. Campden took her leave, upon the whole well satisfied with her reconnaissance.

"That bread-and-cheese business can't last for ever," said she to herself. "Miss Kate will soon come round to common-sense, or else I am much mistaken."

And she wrote a letter to Mr. Holt that very night, bidding him be of good cheer, for that matters were working in the right direction. She had been a matchmaker—having had little else to do —all her life, but she had never entered into any matrimonial plot with such gusto as in this case. The day when she saw Kitty Mrs. Holt, and on which she would be able to say, "That girl owes it all to me," would be indeed a proud one to her. And she saw it now at no great distance.

Her visit left the two sisters, as usual, in greater despondency than it had found them.

"Mrs. Campden's reference to our bread and cheese was in exceedingly bad taste," said Kitty, with unwonted indignation. "I think you deserve great credit, Jenny, for not flying out at her."

"My dear Kitty," returned her sister, "I have had my say, as Mrs. Campden herself calls it, about that woman, and have made up my mind to hold my tongue. Besides, it was *your* bread and cheese, not mine. Do you suppose I don't see how you are starving yourself for my sake?" added she, with a sudden burst of tenderness.

"No, no, darling; I am doing nothing of the kind; I am all right," sobbed Kitty. They were weeping now in each other's arms. "It was very foolish of me to be so angry, but she was cruel to taunt us with our poverty. What can be the good of that?"

"*Good!*" cried Jenny, with passionate contempt. "Do you imagine she ever thinks of 'the good?' She talked like that in order to have an excuse for sending us broken victuals as well as cast-off clothes. Who cares what she says!"

"That is true. It is Uncle George's conduct that

hurts me, not hers.   He ought to have written, or
come over, or something, after that—that letter of
his wife's."

"He is a coward; that is the long and short
of it.   You never showed me that letter, Kitty;
but——"

"I burnt it," interrupted Kate.

"I know you did.   I only wish to ask you one
question about it.   Was there anything in it insulting—I mean disrespectful—to dear papa?"

"There was something about him, not exactly
insulting——"

"I understand; you need say no more, Kitty.
I suspected as much.   If I had known it; well,
things are best as they are; but pray, never let me
meet Mrs. Campden again.   I will not answer for
my tongue, else.   The very sensation of being in
that woman's neighbourhood stifles me."

Nothing more was said on the matter; but
Jenny, notwithstanding her observation that
matters were best as they were, was furious at the
reflection that Mrs. Campden was probably under
the impression that she had seen that communication to Kitty, and yet had not resented its insults to
her father.

The morning after next brought two letters to

the Nook, where now the postman so rarely delivered one.

"Well, Jenny, here is an invitation for us all to go to town!" cried Kitty triumphantly.

"Not from the Skiptons, surely?"

"Well, no; from nobody quite so fashionable. It is from Nurse Haywood, at Islington. Her house is vacant, it seems; and if we would only come and live there till dear papa returns—or—or something turns up. Of course we must not take advantage of the dear creature's kindness as to terms; but even if we paid her a moderate rent, it would, I do believe, be cheaper than living here."

"May I see the letter?—Ah! then you have been writing to her to ask whether we could come, because of what I said to you the other day about my hating to be near Riverside! Oh Kitty, Kitty, you think of everybody but yourself! I know you would dislike living in town in such a different way from what——"

"Indeed, I should not," interposed Kitty, flushing up. She *had* an objection to live in London, but it was certainly not that. She had a vague fear that Mr. Holt would find opportunities of pressing his suit.

"Well, if you really wouldn't mind, Kitty, I *should* so prefer it. And fancy what a pleasure it will be to dear old nurse, and—Jeff!"

Kitty was silent for a little; then quietly said: "There was a letter from Jeff, was there not?"

"Yes, darling; but as you won't show me yours, I won't show you mine—just yet. You are not jealous, are you?"

Either from the idea of leaving Sanbeck, or for some other reason, Jenny was for a wonder in high spirits; and these sometimes, as the phrase goes, carried her away with them.

"No, darling, I am not jealous," answered Kitty gently; "but I thought you told me that you liked being at the Nook because of the old books, which were so useful to you in your writing."

"Did I, dear? Then I was talking nonsense, as I very often do." And again she smiled. It was seldom that she did so; but when she did, the smile gave her delicate intelligent face a rare beauty, and a softness which of late it had sorely lacked.

Kitty kissed her.

"We shall have to sell all our things, Jenny, or most of them, before we can get away quite free from debt, and set up housekeeping again in

London. I suppose they must be sold in Blea-barrow."

"Very good, my dear," answered Jenny cheer-fully. "Write to the auctioneer at once; or shall I write? I know the gentleman, for he made my reclining-couch. I think I made rather a conquest of him, and he may take off that one-eighth per cent. which Jeff has got so much to talk about."

"What a pleasure it is to see you laugh again, Jenny," said Kitty fondly.

"And what a cheap pleasure," answered the other gaily, "which is a great consideration. By-the-bye," added she, with sudden gravity, "there is one debt we have quite forgotten, though I of all people ought to have remembered it—there is the dear old doctor's account to be settled."

The light faded out of her face, which had once more grown bright and young; it was as though a child had suddenly been debarred from some long-promised treat.

"I have been thinking of it a great deal, Jenny. If he charges us as he ought to do, it will be a long bill—because you know there was his attendance upon dear mamma. Still, I am sure, it will be as reasonable as he can justly make it. We must sell a little more of the furniture, that's all. Nurse

Haywood's house has almost everything we shall require, you know."

· " It is a dreadful thing for a poor family to have an invalid in it," said Jenny, in a low voice; " Mrs. Campden was right there."

" Mrs. Campden is never right—at least about *us,*" replied Kitty decisively. " Of course we would have you well if we could; but you are dearer to us as you are, than any one else could be in the rudest health. Now, let us set to work, Jenny, at once, since we really are going away, and forget all our invalid fancies in active employment."

" For which I am so very useful," said Jenny · bitterly.

" There are other and better ways of being useful, my dear, than in cording boxes and carrying them up and down stairs. You can write to the auctioneer, as you suggested, for example; and you can pen a few pretty lines to the doctor, asking him to be so good as to let us know what we owe him; he will like it better coming from you than from me; and besides, you can express yourself ten times as well as I can. It is not a very agreeable task, I fear, my darling."

" It is not worse than things you have to do yourself, Kitty, every hour of the day," answered

Jenny passionately. "You are starving yourself—you are working yourself to the bone, for others; and I won't be spoilt in this way, and treated like a child; I won't indeed."

Kitty opened her large eyes at this outburst; but before she could reply, Jenny had sat down at her mother's desk and seized a pen.

"Don't talk, please," said she, with a sudden change from vexation to mock-gravity, "because I am engaged in business."

The notion of "business" as associated with that fragile and immaterial creature was so utterly incongruous and absurd, that Kitty, whose laughter, fortunately for her, was always much nearer to her lips than the tears to her eyes, could not restrain her mirth.

Both Jenny's letters were answered promptly enough. The auctioneer came over from Bleabarrow in person, appraised the furniture, gave them a rough estimate of what it would fetch, and received his instructions. Everything was to be sold without reserve, except the piano, a few books, and some knickknacks that had belonged to their mother.

Dr. Curzon sent his reply by return of post, to the effect that in case Mr. Dalton should come home with a gold mine in his pocket, he would send them in such a bill as could not be made out without consultation with Dr. Jefferson, who was an expert in that art; but otherwise that they should get no bill from him. His hand, it was true, was against every man and in every man's pocket, he said, but that he did not make war against young ladies. Moreover, that such an idea had been imputed to him had given him mortal offence, which nothing but their all coming to dine with him on the ensuing day could wipe out.

This communication had a very different effect from what the writer had intended; for its recipient broke down as she read it, and gave way to a burst of tears.

Poor Jenny! The hardness of the world made her bitter, and its softness made her weak; or was it the contrast between them that affected her more than either?

But both sisters argued that Dr. Curzon's bill must be paid, and they sent by Tony a few earnest yet graceful words to that effect, as well as an acceptance of the doctor's invitation.

"Your bill shall be sent in," was the reply brought back, along with an intimation that the doctor's "private equipage"—which was in fact the Bleabarrow fly—should be sent for them on the morrow.

Upon the whole, it was a more cheerful little dinner-party than could have been expected. Their host did not seem surprised that they were bent on leaving Sanbeck, though he expressed the regret which, without doubt, he felt upon his own account. Very little was spoken about the Campdens; their host was far from saying anything to widen the breach between the families; but when Kitty spoke of the annoyance which she feared the sale at Bleabarrow would cause at Riverside, he observed drily: "It is generally disagreeable to see folks drown, especially in shallow water; but it is less painful to some people than wetting their own shoes. At all events, I have no sympathy to spare, under such circumstances, for those upon the bank."

Jenny said nothing, but thanked him with her eyes.

She would have been still more grateful to him had she known what happened on the morrow; how the doctor rode up to Riverside, and breaking through that neutrality which it behoves every medical man who practises in the country to maintain, had attempted to plead the Daltons' cause with Mrs. Campden. He lost it, of course, and his temper with it; and in the end gave a piece of his mind to Mr. Campden, who made one in the interview, and about one-tenth of one in the conversation.

His wife had observed that the Dalton girls had behaved disrespectfully to her in coming to this decision about giving up their house without consulting her. "And as for selling their furniture in Bleabarrow, under our very noses, as it were, it is most inconsiderate and disgraceful."

"It is ill-judged, my dear," said Mr. Campden; "but there cannot be any disgrace in selling one's own property to pay one's debts."

"I agree with Mrs. Campden," said the doctor, "that it is very disgraceful."

"There, you see; Dr. Curzon agrees with *me!*" cried the lady triumphantly. "He knows the circumstances, and especially his patient, Miss Jenny's character, who, you may depend upon it, is at the bottom of this. She would do anything to spite me, because I thought it right to set before her sister her true position."

This attack on his favourite Jenny cut the last strand of the doctor's patience.

" Your wife mistakes me, Mr. Campden. I
think it a great disgrace that the sale should take
place ; but the disgrace lies at your door, not theirs.
If I had your money, or one-hundredth part of it,
before I would permit two helpless girls, my
kinswomen, to be sold up——"

" Insolent apothecary !" interrupted Mrs. Campden, shrilly, " how *dare* you ? You know nothing
about the matter. You never had two shillings to
rub against one another. My husband's money,
indeed ! I should like to know what *you* would
do with it ? "

" Well, then, I'll tell you, madam. The very
first thing I would do with it, if I were he—though
it cost me fifty thousand pounds—would be to
get a divorce from my wife." And with that the
doctor clapped his hat on his head, and walked
out of the house, not to enter it again for many
a year.

This little scene did not tend to increase the
cordiality of the tenants of Riverside towards those
of the Nook. It did, in fact, widen the breach
between them exceedingly. When the sale was
over, and it wanted still a week to the time fixed
for the Daltons' departure, Mrs. Campden wrote
a coldly civil letter to Kitty, offering the use of

her carriage to take them to the station. This
Kitty rightly took as a polite hint that a farewell
visit to Riverside might be dispensed with, which
was so far a great relief. At the same time, the
sense that they had been separated so soon and
so utterly from those they had considered their
best friends, by the bare blade of poverty, was
keenly felt. She also trembled to think of the
isolation that had befallen those committed to her
trust. At present, however, thanks to the necessity
for exertion consequent on their departure, this last
consideration did not press so hard upon her ; but
she knew that it was, as it were, in abeyance, to
become cruelly poignant when they should find
themselves in the wild waste of London.

The last hour the two girls and Tony spent
at Sanbeck was passed at their mother's grave.
Workmen of all kinds are tardy in the country,
and the pretty headstone, with its simple "OUR
MOTHER," and the date upon it, had been only just
erected. The doctor met the little pious band
returning from the churchyard, and promised them
that Mrs. Dalton's resting-place should be henceforth his peculiar care. "You must come down
and see the flowers growing upon it, my dears,"
he said. And much else he said, as welcome and

as comforting; how they had yet left to them in the little valley one friend on whom they could count at all times—not very able, but good for something at a pinch, and very, very willing.

" But you have never sent that account you promised, and therefore we don't trust you," said Kitty, severely, wishing to stop Jenny's tears, which were flowing freely.

" I have brought it with me," said he ; and he gave it her. " It is the last remembrance you will have of me, as is the case with all doctors. And now good-bye, darlings."

He rode off on his stout pony as the Riverside carriage came thundering into the courtyard.

There were still a few minutes to spare before parting with old Margate. (The maid, more open-mouthed than ever, was to accompany them as baby's nurse and bottle-holder.) Kitty's housewifely instincts caused her to look at the total of the doctor's " little account."

" Oh Jenny ! " cried she, " what do you think that wicked old dear has done ? "

" Charged us too little, of course—something ridiculously small. I knew he would."

" My dear, he has *receipted* the bill. What are we to do ? "

But Jenny had already left the room, and the last box was being put on the carrier's cart.

"I really am afraid it won't do to pay Dr. Curzon, Jenny," said she, reverting to the subject when they were seated in the carriage. "We must write him a pretty letter of thanks together, instead."

"Yes; he will value that higher than your cheque, Kitty, God bless him."

They did not speak much more together as they drove down the quiet valley where they had left their dear one behind them. Their hearts were too full of memories—and perhaps forebodings.

When they got into the train—a second-class carriage happened, by good fortune, to be empty—Kitty again broke silence.

"What on earth had you to say to Charles, Jenny?" (Charles was the Campdens' footman.) "Of course, I gave something both to him and the coachman."

"Don't be afraid, my dear, of my paying people twice over," returned Jenny, laughing. "I assure you I mean to be as careful of my money as though I were ever so rich. I was only discharging a little debt."

"What debt?"

"The debt we owe to Mrs. Campden—that horrid ten pounds she lent us. If the doctor had taken his dues, I should have felt bound to pay them, so far as I could, out of my privy purse, since the bill was incurred on my account. But *now*—oh, I am so glad to have sent that woman back her ten pounds! I didn't do it insultingly, mind; I just sent a few lines as we were leaving the Nook, to thank her for the use of the carriage —for you know she said she had sent it principally on 'dear Jenny's' account—and enclosed the amount of her late loan. Oh dear, how nice it was! How happy I feel!"

"But, my dear Jenny, where did you *get* the ten pounds?"

"From here," said Jenny, touching her forehead with her forefinger, "from *here*, my dear. I draw upon my imagination, and my imagination draws upon a firm in Paternoster Row which honours its cheques."

CHAPTER IX.

THE SWING OF THE PENDULUM.

LIFE is not all sorrow even to the sorrowful.
There are hours when the sick are well, when
the prisoners are enfranchised, when the poor are
wealthy. It may be that they only seem so by
comparison with their usual lot (for has not happiness been defined by a sad sage as freedom from
pain ?) ; yet they *are* happy ; buoyant, thankful,
believing, for a little while, that the sun shines for
them as well as for others ; that Fate is not, after
all, so hard. Thus it was with the two sisters as
they sat together in the railway carriage, the one
disclosing, the other drinking in, the details of a
literary success.

The baby was asleep, and Tony was endeavouring to teach the open-mouthed maid the rudiments
of travelling piquet. She would count the sheep

per head instead of per flock, and in doing so missed the magpies, the donkeys, and all that was really valuable upon her side of the way.

"This news is wonderful, dear Jenny," cried Kitty, admiringly. "The idea of your being a real live author! I thought that you had some idea of getting money by your lace-work; and so did dear mamma. We used to talk about it together, though we never spoke of it to you, and she used to tremble so lest you should meet with some disappointment. She said people would not think so much of your lace, beautiful as it was, when they had to pay for it."

"She was right, Kitty. I failed in the lace-line; I thought I would try literature."

"Good heavens!" murmured Kitty, overcome with the audacity of this idea.

"Yes, my dear, I said to myself: 'I will be an author.' You know I was always fond of scribbling. I suppose I had written as much as Shakespeare from first to last; though there was a considerable difference in the quality."

"Don't let us say that," said Kitty, encouragingly.

"Well, other people said it, my dear (or the equivalent of it) at all events; editors especially."

"Editors! You write to editors, then?" Kitty regarded her sister with a sublime surprise—an admiration tinctured with awe.

"Why, no; I got Jeff to take the things, and to offer them as though they were his own productions."

"Jeff! You made poor Jeff pretend to be an author! But how *could* he?"

"He went to work as naturally as possible. He gave them tragedy, comedy, melodrama, and sentimental effusions; but no one ever expressed a doubt."

"How charming!" exclaimed Kitty, clapping her hands together in joyful excitement. "And they were all accepted, of course?"

"No, dear; they were all rejected. The editors told Jeff that he must have patience, and 'fill his basket.' (The expression puzzled him a good deal, by-the-bye; he said he had only heard of one's 'bread-basket,' and how was an author to fill *that*, if he could not sell his works.) He was to read more, they meant, and not attempt to spin things out of himself, like a spider. You shall read Jeff's description of it all some day. So I set to work upon Mr. Landell's library. It was rather dry work at first; but I ferreted out some curious and out-of-the-way things, and made two articles out of them, and told Jeff to try his fortune with them with 'The Smellfungus Magazine.' And the editor actually accepted them."

"Only to think of it, Jenny! Then you were in print! And yet you never told us! How could you keep such a secret, and oh, Jenny, from dear mamma, too, whom it would have pleased so much!"

"I have often thought of that, dear," answered the other, gravely; "but it does not matter now. What I had set my heart on was to get money for us all—to show that I was not going to be the clog and the burden to you that—that woman at Riverside took it for granted I should be. And since for those articles I got no money, I determined to say nothing about them. But Jeff—dear Jeff—so managed it that for a story I wrote, all out of these old materials, I did get money. The day you heard from Nurse Haywood he sent me two five-pound notes from the editor. I should have given them to you at once, only you spoke of Dr. Curzon's bill, and I thought they ought to go towards *that*. Even so, it would have been very nice; but as it is—to have paid Mrs. Campden off with them—it is simply delicious! We are out of debt,

and we shall have the means of livelihood. This
was 'the hope' that I told that woman we still had,
and at which you smiled so sadly, when she came
to call that day at the Nook: the hope of my being
able to make money by my pen; and you see it has
been realised. It is not such a bad world, after all;
if only dear papa comes home to us. I think he
will come now; I do indeed. Everything looks so
much brighter, though I thought we were never to
have a ray of sunshine again. Kiss me, Kitty."

The two girls sat locked in a close embrace.

"But, Jenny, why did you let us leave Sanbeck? You will no longer have any books to—
to——"

"To 'gut.' That was the word the editor used
to Jeff, little knowing that he was giving advice to
a lady. He said that at the British Museum I
should find any amount of old books to—to per-
form that operation upon. It seems I have a
talent for evisceration."

"I daresay," said Kitty, confidently, "though I
don't know what it means. It seems to me you
have a talent for everything. Oh, you dear, clever
creature!" cried she, holding her at arm's-length,
"I declare I feel quite afraid of you; I shall never
dare scold you again."

In the exuberance of her admiration, Kitty must needs confide the fact of Jenny's authorship to Tony, but without awakening the like enthusiasm, for that gentleman being deep in his game of travelling piquet, which disinclined him to withdraw his attention from external objects, and also not being particularly interested in literary matters, only observed that " Jenny was a stunner, and that he had always said so." And if he had been informed that she had been made editress of "The Quarterly Review," or "Punch," or both, he would probably have made the same observation.

This philosophy upon Tony's part, with which Kitty was herself inclined to quarrel, amused Jenny exceedingly, and for an hour or two she continued in the highest spirits. Then the long travel and comparative discomfort of the carriage began to tell upon her feeble frame; she grew pale with pain and weariness, then sick and faint. They were fortunately still alone, and all was done for her in the way of affectionate tendance that could be done. Kitty was not one of those young ladies who associate faintness with immediate dissolution, and are frightened out of their small wits on beholding an attack of illness; but she felt with anguish that the improvement which was hoped had taken place of late in her sister's health must have been less real than apparent. Perhaps those very attempts to procure money by her pen, over which they had just been so sanguine, had exhausted and enfeebled her. At this thought the momentary sunshine in poor Kitty's heart was quite extinguished, and the clouds that covered it were darker than those it had dispelled. What were a few pounds earned now and again, when set against the cost of Jenny's life? As the light faded out from the short winter's day, and she sat with Jenny's aching head pillowed on her breast, and with the baby's feeble moan in her ears, she was filled with sad forebodings; strange thoughts of self-sacrifice and self-negation, which had for a time grown unfamiliar to her, retook possession of her brain, and turned her cold—as cold, but as steady, as a statue. As the whistle sounded, and the train plunged into the last tunnel, she pictured to herself her last return from Riverside, alone, when Jenny and her mother had come to meet her at the station and take her home. Now there was no mother, nor any home that could be called such; and none to meet, or——

"Kitty! Jenny!—there's Jeff!" cried Tony, excitedly, as the carriage glided into the gas-lit station. And in another moment Jeff's hand was on the door, and his bright face smiled through the window-pane, as he ran beside the still moving train.

How glad, and yet how sad, Kitty felt to see him; glad upon her sister's account, to whom she could now entirely devote herself, while Jeff looked after the baggage; but sad upon her own, for somehow his presence scattered and broke down those "low beginnings of content" she had begun to feel in that scheme of self-sacrifice which she had just now been painfully elaborating. Oh, why had he come with his kind tones and tender eyes, ere yet her mind had had time to harden in its mould of duty!

"Jenny is very tired, Jeff," was all her greeting to him, except the thankful pressure of her fingers.

"Of course she is," returned he, cheerfully. "How could it be otherwise after such a journey! I have got a brougham for her, so that she should not be jolted quite to pieces. So get you into it, you three folks and a half; and I will follow with Tony and the baggage in a four-wheeler."

"A brougham!" sighed Jenny, looking more dead than alive. "I call that a wasteful extravagance."

"Pooh, pooh!" he whispered; "distinguished authoresses don't ride about in hack-carriages in London, let me tell you, whatever they may do in Sanbeck."

No further expostulation was made, for indeed nothing could have been more welcome to poor Jenny's back and limbs than the cushions of the vehicle in question, which Jeff had had supplemented for her especial use. She felt positively better on her arrival in Brown Street, after their long drive through miscalled "Merry Islington"—the dullest and drabbest of all suburbs—than when she had left the train. She had been as eloquent about Jeff's thought and kindness on the way as her feeble voice would permit her to be; but Kitty had answered nothing. She knew how tender and how true he was, and dared not trust herself to praise him. To her great relief, he did not present himself that night in Brown Street, but left the little family to "settle down" in their new dwelling alone. If it was not "like home," it was very unlike what ordinary lodgings would have been; instead of the smiles of a mercenary landlady, there was the honest, kind face of Nurse Haywood to give them welcome. It would not have beamed half so brightly had they been rich folks who had agreed " for six months certain " at treble the rent; for she loved " the young ladies " as though they had been her own children, and thought them the most beautiful and charming of God's creatures. " Master Tony " had always been her especial darling; and the baby she regarded as a precious and sacred charge bequeathed by its sainted mother to the world, in compensation for her departure heavenward.

Kitty always used to assert that Nurse Haywood was " a lady; " and looking at her with her neat gray hair, and gentle, quiet face, as she stood dressed in her new black silk, to welcome the bereaved ones, you would have endorsed that opinion.

She wore a certain gold watch and chain a little ostentatiously, to be sure, in the front of her dress, but then these had been given her by Mr. Dalton's own hand, and she wished to show herself mindful of him. Her face, like her person, was plump, and, notwithstanding her advanced years, quite free from wrinkles; and if her voice was somewhat broken, it was not through age, but because, though old, she had retained all her sympathies and affections (the more easily, perhaps, that they were within narrow limits), and was sadly "upset" at the sight of her dear ones. It was their trouble that troubled her; and her chief care and fear were that, accustomed as they were, as she expressed it, "to the best of everything," the accommodation she had to offer them in Brown Street would seem miserable and insufficient.

The sight of Jenny, so wan and travel-worn, utterly overcame her, and she could only exclaim, "My poor, *poor* lamb!" as she folded her to her heart.

Truly the "wind was tempered" to her and to all the shorn flock in that hospitable dwelling. It was humble, yet, as Kitty shrewdly suspected, by no means so low-rented as the price Nurse Haywood had charged them. They would be none the less a burden on their old friend, because she would bear it like a feather; and if it lasted long, how *could* she bear it! However, she drove those thoughts away, and for the present resolved to feel only thankfulness. After the nice little supper, at which Tony greatly distinguished himself, and which she herself did her best to swallow, lest her hostess should ascribe her want of appetite to fastidiousness; and after she had seen the rest of the party stowed away in their small dormitories, and Jenny, dead-tired, had fallen asleep, Kitty sat

down in her room, over an unaccustomed fire, to
cast up the expenses of the day. Accounts had of
old been hateful to her, but now she found a refuge
in them from thought. Their dry details shut out
alike reflection on the past and forebodings for the
future.

Scarcely had she begun, however, when there
was a gentle knock at the door, and there entered
Nurse Haywood.

"Now, my dear Miss Kitty," said she, perceiving
the nature of her occupation, "why on earth are
you a-worriting yourself about pounds and shillings, instead of getting ready for your bed, which,
Heaven knows, you must want enough?"

"But, my dear nurse," answered Kitty, smiling,
"I must needs look after not only pounds and
shillings now, but shillings and pence. You have
endeavoured to spoil us, as usual, with all sorts of
luxuries, this fire in my bedroom for one. But,
indeed, you must not go on so. I told you in my
letter how very different things were with us,
remember."

"I know that, and the more shame to them as
have brought it about." Nurse Haywood firmly
believed that the Daltons' misfortunes had been
caused by some wicked human agency, assisted by

the more or less direct assistance of the devil.
" But you have no call to fash yourself with
money matters yet a while. There's near upon a
hundred pounds, my dear, in the savings bank,
which is yours if it is anybody's, Heaven knows,
since it was all saved in your service."

" Nurse, nurse, don't talk like that! " cried
Kitty, breaking down in spite of herself. " Do
you think we have come here to live upon your
savings ? "

" You are come here to be comfortable and
not to worrit," returned the old dame decisively.
" Your dear papa will be home soon, please God;
and a pretty thing it will be if he finds you have
been denying yourself things in my house. And
even if he don't come back, do you suppose you
have no friends ? "

" None but you, dear nurse; except one or two
who have all the will, indeed, but not the power to
serve us."

" Well, I don't know; gentlemen who ride on
horseback with their groom behind them, have
generally money to spare; and one such at least
has been here to-day to ask after you all. A more
civil-spoken gentleman, or who showed himself more
kindly towards you all, it is not easy to picture."

"'What was the gentleman's name? Was it Sir William Skipton?'"

"Very like, miss. He might have been all that, to judge by his hat and boots, which you might have seen yourself in, just as in that looking-glass. He didn't leave his name; but he said he was a friend of your father's—which went to my heart at once, as you may credit. And he asked after you all, one by one, down to the sweet baby. He thought you had come yesterday, it seems, and called to inquire how you all were after your long journey."

"Was he a little man, with gray whiskers?"

"Oh no, Miss Kitty: he was a tall, fine-looking gentleman, rather stiffish, I should have said, if he had not been so affable. I am sure *he* is a friend of yours, whoever isn't. But what I came up to say was that here is a letter for you, as came by the last post to-day, but which the sight of your sweet faces put clean out of my old head till now. I thought I'd bring it up—else you had much better not read it to-night—in case it was anything about —about your dear papa."

"It is nothing about papa, I am sure," said Kitty, quietly, having cast her eye on the address. "And I shall take your advice, nurse, and go to bed."

She at once proceeded to put away her accounts; and after a cordial " good night," the old dame withdrew. Then Kitty drew her chair to the fire, and gazed at the still closed letter with hard, despairing eyes. She had recognised the handwriting at once as that of Mr. Holt; and she thought she could guess at the nature of its contents. He had called in person, it seemed, that very day, and now he had written her a letter. Fate was not only hard with her but urgent, as though she had already tendered her submission to it.

The envelope was a large one, and held something weighty, like that she had received from Mrs. Campden. Was it possible that this man had dared to send her money—bank-notes? No; thank heaven! it was not that. There was a letter, and something official on a large piece of paper. The receipt of a premium from a life insurance office for one hundred and twenty pounds. What could it mean? The letter was of course from Mr. Holt.

" MY DEAR MISS DALTON,—In the hurry of your father's departure from England he omitted to pay his usual premium to the *Palm Branch*. As in a few days it would have been overdue, and the policy thereby have lapsed, I have taken the liberty to guard against that contingency. The money has been paid under protest—that is to say, if it should turn out—which Heaven forbid!—that your poor father should have deceased before this date the society will repay the premium in question, together with the policy of five thousand pounds. You will perceive, therefore, that I have incurred no risk, nor yourself any obligation, by this transaction, which I have only effected as a mere matter of convenience to you, and of course not without consultation with your friends.

"I did myself the honour to call in Brown Street to-day, but mistook, it seems, the date of your arrival in town. Pray, make my best compliments to your sister, and remember me most kindly to my young friend Tony. The acquaintance of the remaining member of your family I have not as yet had the pleasure to make, but I hope he bore his journey with equanimity.— Believe me, my dear Miss Dalton, yours always most faithfully,   RICHARD HOLT."

She took up the receipt again and read it with scarlet check. "Received one hundred and twenty pounds." She was indebted, therefore, in that sum—or in nearly a whole year's income—to the man who paid it; and when he wrote that no obligation had been incurred on her part, he was writing an untruth, and one which he knew could not impose upon her for a moment. The "friends" with whom he had consulted were, of course, the Campdens, or probably only Mrs. Campden. Surely "Uncle George" could never have allowed himself to be a party to a scheme which made her this man's debtor.

She had not known the money was due. The application, in fact, had come through her father's bankers, who had been duly instructed to pay it; and since there were now no funds in hand, they had forwarded it to Riverside. How hopeless would she have felt at Sanbeck, had she been aware of it; and how hopeless she felt now! Even if her father should come home to-morrow —poorer, in all probability, than he went—she would be none the less indebted to Mr. Holt. Indeed, the certain news of her father's death, and the consequent payment of his policy, could alone acquit her of the pecuniary obligation, let alone any other. Oh, cruel fate! that her only escape from an unwelcome—she dared not now say even to herself, now that the thing might come to pass, a detested—suitor, should be, as it were, over her father's corpse !

She could of course decline to receive this help at all; could object to the premium being paid at all; but then there was the contingency which Mr. Holt had glanced at, of her father dying after the premium had become overdue. He might be wrecked somewhere at that moment, but still alive; and yet he might not come back alive to England. In that case his children would lose the policy : that five thousand pounds, the possession or loss of which would make all the difference to them for their lives in this world; would insure them competence, or condemn them to the poverty that one at least of them was so ill-fitted to bear.

That very morning—not twelve hours ago—Kitty had been happy, hopeful, in her sister's triumph; now it seemed an age since happiness had visited her, and, moreover, that it would never visit her again. Her future looked dark indeed. The self-sacrifice she was contemplating was one which no man can estimate; there is nothing like it in the experience of his sex; for when a man marries a woman for her money, it is she, and not himself, when all is said, who in truth is sacrificed.

In many cases, indeed, such as poor Kitty's, the gilded chain soon ceases to gall; it is only a few to whom romance is necessary, and the purchased bride finds her life very tolerable; but Kitty was conscious of an obstacle to her self-abnegation, which made it ten times more hard for her, and almost a crime. In giving herself to Richard Holt, she was casting away the offer of Geoffrey Derwent's love; and in her heart of hearts she had accepted it.

"Oh mother, mother!" cried she despairingly, as she turned upon her sleepless bed, "why, why did you leave me!"

. She had never felt the need of an adviser and a comforter so much as now.

CHAPTER X.

BROWN STREET is not lovely, but it is far from being so melancholy a place of residence as that wherein three-fourths of the population of London are doomed to pass their lives. There was light in it and air enough, at least for persons in good health; and at the end of it, where the builder's money had come to an end, and he went into the Bankruptcy Court, there was still a space unoccupied by brick and mortar, through which a glimpse of the country could be seen. This was not the valley of Sanbeck, but it was open ground, with a spectral tree or two, holding its ragged arms aloft, as though in deprecation of the advancing host of houses; and afar off was what looked like a village church—though it was, in fact, the tower of a Waterworks Company. The dwellings in Brown Street were

clean, at least externally—at Mrs. Haywood's you
could have " eaten your dinner off the floor," it was
so spick and span—and they had not yet begun to
" peel," to exhibit those cracks and flakes peculiar to stucco, which is analogous to some skin
diseases in the human frame.   The street was situated between two magnets, or would-be magnets.
There was an immense public-house at one end,
which had not yet succeeded in withdrawing the
custom of the humbler classes from the old pot-
house in the neighbourhood, but was convenient
for those who liked their beer on draught, and
were not very particular as to what it was made of ;
and at the other end was an ecclesiastical edifice of
iron, about which the pious part of the population
had not quite made up their minds.   Service was
performed there every Sunday by a real clergyman ;
but one likes one's church to *look* like a church,
and it might not afford that security against fire—
in the end—which its material suggested.   From
Brown Street ran off at right angles Little Brown
Street, a spot devoted to the hatching of small
shops of all descriptions, about half of which were
addled ; or rather the thing that was brought forth
—it was chiefly in the cheap newspaper and tobacco
line, the toy line, or the cheap tailoring line (with

a splendid picture of the Fashions in the window,—lived but a week or two; it sparkled, was
exhausted, and went to the brokers. The omni-
buses—one line of them, at all events—knew of
the existence of Brown Street, because commercial
gents of various kinds lodged there, and were
"taken up" every morning within a few hundred
yards of it; but the cabs ignored it. "Brown
Street? Where was Brown Street? Might it be
down away by the Duke of York's Head, ma'am?"
A question no lady fare could answer. One may
imagine, therefore, how entirely unknown it was
to "carriage people." Yet on the very day after
the arrival of the Dalton family, the equipage of no
less a person than Lady Skipton did somehow
contrive to find its way there. "Never heerd of
sich a place, my lady," said the coachman to his
mistress, when directed to drive thither. "Never
seed sich a place," was his remark, in confidence,
to the footman, as the carriage bumped over the
half-formed roads, and over the broken bricks that
plentifully strewed it; "it's a cruelty to a carridge
and 'osses."

Jenny was not visible to her ladyship: after that
episode of the lacework, she would not have seen
her under any circumstances, but on this occasion

she was really too ill to do so. The journey had utterly knocked her up. So Kitty received her alone. She was far from well herself, for she had had but little sleep; and she had been thinking all the morning what sort of reply she should write to Mr. Holt's letter. But she felt that she was not in a position to refuse to see anybody who might be of service to them. It was a sickening thought that even her friendships—as she had been accustomed to call them—must now be alloyed with views of self-interest. With Lady Skipton came her daughter Leonora—Lenny, as Kitty was wont to call her—who had attended classes with her in old days, and, next to Mary Campden, had been her greatest confidante. She was a pleasant little person, with a great deal of hair and a fairy figure. Everybody wondered how such an elephantine mamma—her ladyship weighed about eighteen stone—could have produced such a gazelle. She was one of twins, her sister having died in infancy, or she would probably have been double the size. She had written poems; one, "To my *Alter Ego* in Heaven," was very much admired in her family circle. Kitty had always believed in her sensibility, and defended it against Jenny, who derided her ("She is too much 'up,' Kitty; like ginger-beer "); but somehow she now mistrusted Lenny's impassioned greeting.

"You got my letter, my darling, of course ?" said this young lady.

She had indited one to Sanbeck upon the death of Mrs. Dalton, full of quotations from the poets, and which had jarred on Kitty's sorrow-laden ear. It had been a relief to her that Lenny had written "Don't reply," the one piece of true consideration in the letter.

"How terribly you must have suffered," she went on. "How pale you look, darling."

"Black never becomes the complexion," said Lady Skipton, encouragingly. "When she is in colours again, she will look more like herself. I am so sorry about poor Jenny ; but doubtless the change of air will do her good. I am afraid she was annoyed with me about her lacework ; she sent back the little present I enclosed to her."

Then for the first time Kitty learnt the story of the unsold lace.

"She never mentioned the matter to me, Lady Skipton," answered she, when it had been related to her.

"Come, then, let us hope she was not offended," replied her ladyship cheerfully. "I hope you will

both come and dine with us, as soon as you get
settled, my dear; of course it is a little *soon*," said
she, with a glance at Kitty's mournful garb, "but
then we are old friends."

"I am afraid we shall not be great diners-out
for the future," said Kitty.

"Now don't you go and shut yourselves up, my
dear," replied her ladyship promptly. "In *your*
case particularly, it would be most injudicious. I
won't promise to send the carriage, because Robert
is so particular about his horses; he is in the worst
of tempers at this moment, because there is a
brick or two in the road: but when you come in
a cab, mind, that is always *my* affair. I should
never forgive myself if I caused you any expense,
just now; though I have good reason to believe
that the little inconvenience you may now be
suffering from will soon be over."

"I am glad to hear it," said Kitty, coldly, almost
defiantly, "though it is news to me."

"Well, well, perhaps I am premature; I thought,
from something that dropped from Mrs. Campden—— But no matter. I hope our horses—by-
the-bye, they are old friends of yours, Kitty, for Sir
William bought them of your papa—are not catch-

ing cold. Lenny, just see where Robert has taken
the carriage to."

Lenny looked out of the window and reported
progress in the direction of the public-house.

" I thought so," said her ladyship with irritation.
"Well, my dear, you see we didn't lose a day in
calling on you. By-the-bye, you have never shown
us that dear delightful baby. Is it like your poor
mamma, or who ?"

"The baby is asleep," said Kitty.

"Bless it !" cried Lenny, clasping her little
hands ecstatically. " What is its pretty name ?"

" John. He is called after dear papa."

" Very right, very proper," said Lady Skipton.
" If I had had a boy, I had made up my mind to
call it after his *papa*; though, to be sure, when there
is a title in a family, the thing becomes imperative.
Little Tony, of course, is at school ?"

" No ; he is at home for the present."

" Well, well; I daresay you are wise. So long
as you can exercise authority over a boy, he is best
among home influences. Come, there is Robert at
last; he is wiping his mouth with the back of his
hand, so one knows what *he's* been after. My dear
girl, I do assure you it is not altogether a disadvan-

tage to have to drop your carriage; that man's the
plague of my life.   God bless you ! "

Kitty submitted to an impassioned caress from
Lenny ; and then, to her great relief, the visit was
over. She felt a secret conviction that it was *pour
prendre congé*; and it proved correct. Lady Skipton's invitation to dinner was repeated, after a considerable interval; but she found it impossible—on
account of Robert—to bring her carriage again to
Brown Street. Her afternoon's adventure in the
wilds of Islington gave her a subject for conversation for many a day, with opportunities for dwelling
upon her favourite topic, the abominable behaviour
of her coachman, and for delicately hinting at her
own patronage of friends in reduced circumstances.
" I was not going to desert those dear girls because
they happened to live in Islington ; but what I went
through to see them I shall not easily forget.   The
people stared at us as though we were a travelling
circus ; I don't think a carriage was ever seen in the
neighbourhood before ; and Robert was in the sulks
for a month afterwards !"   Sir William sent Kitty
a brace of partridges and a hare from his country-
seat.   There would have been more, wrote his
wife, but that the birds were so wild that year in
Berkshire.

When Kitty went upstairs, she found Jenny had not yet risen, although she had announced her intention of doing so.

" I felt a little giddy, Kitty, so I thought I'd be lazy. And I write in bed in pencil just as well."

"Pray don't think of writing, Jenny," implored her sister. "You are quite feverish, and your eyes are ever so much brighter than they ought to be."

" That is because I am so anxious to hear about those dear Skiptons," laughed Jenny. " Was her ladyship affable, notwithstanding that we live in Brown Street? I am bound to say I didn't expect her to come and see us. Lenny, of course, was as gushing as ever. She will write a poem about us, called 'Friends, though Fallen,' or some such title: I can see her at it."

" I daresay they meant well, Jenny; but I must confess that it was all rather unsatisfactory."

" Then it must have been very bad indeed," said Jenny.

" Well, they didn't even ask to see poor Tony, though they knew he was in the house, and you know Tony used to call Lenny 'his wife,' for years."

" Ah, you see we can't be too particular—or too little particular—about young gentlemen who are not eligible. The simple fact is, my dear," said Jenny, dropping her tone of raillery, "the Skiptons are rubbish. Our position is that of a sieve, through which we find our sham friends are all dropping out. Nurse Haywood, Dr. Curzon, and Jeff, remain to us; but the rest are all in the dust-heap. Let them lie there. I feel that we shall henceforward be independent of them. I am satisfied—weighing one thing with another, and not even taking into consideration the fact, that dear papa's society has been a sunshine among all these shady people, for which they will always owe him gratitude — that we are indebted to them for nothing. For the future, let us be careful to incur no obligations."

Kitty's heart sank within her; she had Mr. Holt's letter, with his receipt for the premium, at that very moment in her pocket; and Lady Skipton's hateful words—" Any little inconvenience you may now be suffering, I have good reason to believe, from something that dropped from Mrs. Campden, will soon be over"—were still ringing in her ears.

"Above all things," continued Jenny, "I am thankful to think we have got rid of Mr. Holt. To tell you the honest truth, I had really begun to think, dear Kitty, that from some mistaken notions of duty to your family, you might have been induced to listen to that man. Of course, you could never have liked him. What? *You don't say that?*"

"Why *should* I say it, Jenny? He has certainly shown himself well-disposed towards us."

"Yes; but for reasons of his own. Of course he wishes to ingratiate himself with *you*. But do you suppose he has fallen in love with me, and Tony, and the baby also? I saw through that man—I flatter myself—from the first; and I see him—in my mind's eye, Horatio—to the end. Shall I tell you what I see?"

"No, Jenny. I don't wish to hear it. Besides, you are exciting yourself; and I am quite sure that quiet is what you want. Pray, do not try to write to-day." She took the pencil and paper from Jenny's hand, who gave them up without resistance.

"Perhaps you are right, darling: I will let my brains lie fallow for a day or two; they seem all in a muddle, somehow."

Kitty had never seen her sister looking so ill since they had left Riverside. The excitement she had lately gone through, combined with the

M 2

fatigue of travel, had evidently much affected her.
Instead of being the prop and stay she fondly
hoped to be, it was more probable she was about
to be seriously ill.   Dr. Curzon had always said:
"Jenny is progressing, and that is well, for standing still in her case is impossible; there must be
improvement, or else retrogression, which would
be dangerous.   Her constitution is deficient in
rallying power."   The plain English of that professional expression was only too clear to Kitty.

Here, then, was another and urgent reason why
she should make up her mind to accept Mr. Holt's
assistance; yet, in doing so, she felt that she would
be accepting so much more, that it gave her pause.
Jeff was sure to call that evening on his way
home from office, for he lodged close by; and
she resolved—not to consult him; no, him least
of all men; but to ask him one question before
answering Mr. Holt's letter.   After that she would
take her own way in the matter, without seeking
advice from anyone.

As she was taking her frugal supper with Tony
—for the housekeeping was now in her own hands
—Jeff arrived.   She felt a disinclination to be
alone with him, born of her mistrust in her own
fortitude; her heart was wax towards him, and

melted at his presence, though she was so resolved he should not mould it.

"Jeff," whispered she, while Tony was engaged with a new book his friend had bought him, "tell me the truth about dear papa. Is there any hope of his coming back to us?"

"There is always hope, Kitty," replied he, gravely.

"Where there is life," she answered. "But is there life? Is there any chance of his being alive?"

Jeff did not answer, only beat softly with his fingers on the table, and looked most miserable.

"You are loath to give me pain," she said. "I would not put you to pain unless there was a necessity for it. Dear papa has insured his life for our sakes. Is it worth while to pay the premium which has become due?"

"Oh yes," returned the young fellow, eagerly. "You can pay it under protest—that is, supposing that the policy should have fallen due already; in which case you will get the money back again. And then you will make all sure. It is clearly the right thing to do, if—if—it can be done."

"It can be done," returned Kitty, gravely. No more was said upon the subject. When Jeff was gone, and all the inmates of this little house, save herself, were fallen asleep, and freed from earthly cares, Kitty sat down and wrote her answer to Richard Holt. In her own name, and for herself, she thanked him for the payment of the premium. She spoke of it as a loan, of course, but expressed her sense of his generosity as well as of his forethought. She would not pretend that there was, as he suggested, no obligation; she would not affect to understand that his kindness had not herself for its object. She would never encourage him; nay, she would temporise and procrastinate as much as she could; but her weapons—weak though she felt herself to be—should be at least fair weapons, and therefore hypocrisy could not make one of them. Many women will deceive and cajole even those they love; but this one was truthful to the man who, in her secret heart, was hateful to her.

CHAPTER XI.

THE post flies quickly in town, and the next after-noon brought a letter from Mr. Holt, in reply to Kitty's, and asking permission to call on the ensuing day. She was well aware of the signifi-cance of this request; he had called already without permission; but this would be altogether a different sort of visit; one wherein she could not deny nor excuse herself to him, and which would be paid to her alone. Even should he not ask the question upon which she knew he had so resolutely set his mind, this interview would be the forerunner to it, and in permitting it, she must needs foreshadow her reply.

To think was torture; to delay was vain. She sat down, and wrote a few words at once to say that she should be at home at the hour he had named.

The interval, which she had expected to pass in apprehensions of his arrival, was spent in fears of another kind. Jenny grew much worse, so bad that, in spite of her (for Jenny had small confidence in unknown doctors), Kitty yielded to Nurse Haywood's advice, and called in the nearest practitioner.

"Aggravated febrile symptoms; nervous debility; and great cerebral excitement," was his account of the patient. (He talked like a medical handbook, but he was by no means ignorant of his business.) "The young lady requires quiet—freedom from anxiety of all sorts. How does she chiefly employ herself?" asked he, of Kitty.

"In reading and writing."

"You mean by writing, composition? I thought so. The very worst thing for her in her present condition. Reading she must have in moderation; but pen and ink must be kept from her. And as soon as she is fit to be moved, I should recommend sea-air."

Kitty bowed in assent—she believed him the more because Jenny had always been recommended "Brighton" in the spring—and blushing, tendered him one of her ten guineas.

"You have not lived in Brown Street long," he

said, smiling. "Science is cheaper here than in some places." And he returned her thirteen shillings and sixpence. Freedom from greed is one of the many virtues of the medical calling; but to poor Kitty this seemed only another proof how pitiful must be the case of her and hers, since even strangers compassionated it, and returned her money.

"Perfect rest" and "sea-air." The prescription was doubtless good, but could only be carried out in one way—at her own proper cost. If she had hitherto entertained a doubt of the sort of reception that she should give to Mr. Holt, she had none now. And yet things did not happen quite as she expected.

Mr. Holt came indeed with the punctuality of clockwork, but matters had become by that time so serious with Jenny, that little else could be alluded to.

"I am very much shaken and unnerved," said Kitty pleadingly; "you must forgive me if I do not acknowledge your late kindness as it deserves."

"It deserves nothing," returned Mr. Holt. "I hope you will not pain me by alluding to such a *bagatelle.*" (He *would* air his French, even to her.)

" But if I can be of real use, pray, command me.
Now, with respect to Brighton——"

"My sister cannot be moved for weeks," interrupted Kitty quickly; "she is very, very ill."

" Still, when she *can*, I adjure you to remember
that the means will not be wanting. If your father
were—were in England, do you suppose he would
spare any expense for such an object ? A hundred
pounds, or a thousand; what does it matter ? We
have a saying in the City that 'money may be
bought too dear,' but that does not apply to life."

His manner was most respectful, and yet
tender; he took her hand in his, and pressed it
as he said the words, " Money may be bought
too dear," which was inopportune, to say the least
of it. But she did not withdraw her hand.

" I entreat you," he went on, " not to add to
your real sorrow, by worrying yourself about
pecuniary troubles; for so long as Richard Holt
is alive they are visionary. I shall send or call
to inquire daily; but I shall not intrude upon you
while your sister remains so indisposed—unless it
would be any relief to you to see me," added he,
with gentle pleading.

" You are very, very good," said Kitty. " I am
not fit to see any one just now."

If he had hoped for any other answer, he did not show it. His behaviour was the perfection of patience and devotion. Kitty would have felt really sorry for him—as her mother had done—if she had not been so wretched on her own account. It was impossible to doubt that the man loved her; and to be loved without return is almost as bad (to a kind heart) as to love under the like circumstances.

"Did you walk?" inquired she, mustering some show of interest in him, as he took his leave.

"No; I rode: my horse is at the corner of the street. I left it there because Mr. Derwent told me that your sister was so ill, and I feared the noise would disturb her."

This was thoughtful of him in one way, but he was foolish to have mentioned Jeff; it somehow stopped her thanks.

"Good-bye," he said, "my dear Miss Dalton; or rather, I should say *au revoir.*"

He came the next day and the next, but had no speech with Kitty. Her place was by her sister's pillow, and she could not leave it. Thus once more it happened that by a caprice of Fate she was saved by one species of misery from the endurance of another. Weeks went by without much

alteration in the condition of the sick girl; and
then the spring came, and with it a little renewed
vigour. In the meantime her story had appeared
in "The Smellfungus Magazine," and achieved what
in the periodical world is held to be a success. A
second edition of that serial—the first had not
been a very large one—had been called for in
consequence. Mr. Sanders had written to Jeff a
cautiously expressed letter of congratulation, be-
speaking a "more sustained work" from the same
"gifted pen, combining fiction with antiquarian
details."

"The beggar takes me for Walter Scott," was
Jeff's observation. Yet he could hardly smile at
this new proof of the editor's misplaced confidence,
for he knew that many a month must pass away
before she, whose representative he was, could
resume her pen, even if she could ever do so.

He wrote to say that indisposition would in-
capacitate him for the present from writing for
"The Smellfungus;" and the next day Mr. Sanders
met him at luncheon-time in a City oyster-shop,
eating like Dando and drinking stout.

"You are writing for something else, you know
you are," exclaimed the editor with a burst of irritation. "I should have thought the author of

'The Monk of Monkwearmouth ' [Jenny's successful tale] had been more of a gentleman.''

"He is nothing of the kind, and never made any pretensions to it," said Jeff coolly.

Mr. Sanders thought him more like Chatterton than ever.

One morning, Mr. Holt received a telegram, which, as was usual with him, he opened in Jeff's presence. His table was covered with letters every morning, yet he received more telegrams than letters, and none of these various communications ever seemed to move him. But on this occasion he leant back in his chair, and turned deadly pale.

"Are you ill, sir?" said Jeff with interest.

"I feel a little faint: it is the spring weather. Get me a draught of water."

When Jeff brought the glass, the telegram had disappeared, and his employer was consulting "Bradshaw."

"I shall have to go away from office to-day," said he, speaking more thickly than his wont. "I have been summoned to—Plymouth. There will be no business of any importance to transact, I believe."

"Very good, sir. In case any one wishes to see you, when shall I say you will be back?"

Mr. Holt did not answer. He seemed to be in difficulties with his "Bradshaw," a work which he had generally at his fingers' ends.

"Tell the boy to fetch me a cab—a hansom," said he presently. "There is not a minute to lose," added he, as if to himself. Then, before Jeff could leave the room, his employer uttered so terrible an execration that the young fellow turned to look at him in astonishment. He had never heard him swear before, and it really seemed as though he were making up for past omissions in that respect. Mr. Holt's usually calm face had become a sea of passion.

"I said *a cab*," exclaimed he imperiously. Jeff himself flew for a hansom, and as he caught one passing the archway out of the court, Mr. Holt was at his heels. He did not seem to notice him, and perhaps took him for the office boy, as he leaped into the vehicle.

"King's Cross—and drive like the devil," was his direction to the cabman. And the man drove off at the pace supposed to be affected by his Satanic majesty.

In his hurry and passion, had his employer given the wrong address? thought Jeff; or had his statement that he was going to Plymouth been an untruth? Certainly King's Cross was not the station for that town.

He had left his letters behind him unopened—even those from Liverpool, where he had a small branch establishment, and which generally claimed his first attention. Something serious had certainly occurred.

At eleven o'clock arrived Mr. Dawkins, a pretty frequent visitor in Abdell Court. He appeared greatly excited; his neckcloth, always tight for his large throat, seemed almost to suffocate him, making his face to swell and his eyes to project in a very alarming manner. "Where is your master?" inquired he hurriedly.

"Do you mean Mr. Holt?" replied Jeff with stiffness. "He is gone away. A telegram arrived for him this morning which took him out of town."

"Ay; to Liverpool, of course," said Mr. Dawkins. "Then the news is true, I suppose?"

"What news?"

"Look here, my young fellow," said Mr. Dawkins persuasively, "everybody must know it by this evening, and before your employer comes back: it is a question of hours. You cannot possibly do any harm by telling me just 'Yes or No' about the *Flamborough Head*. I can make it well worth your while;" and he tapped his breast-pocket, which was always bulging with bank-notes.

Jeff looked at him severely. "No!" roared he. He was very angry, but he knew that words—as a vehicle for moral sentiments at least—would be wasted upon Mr. Dawkins.

"Do you mean that the news isn't true, or that you won't take the money?" asked Mr. Dawkins.

"I don't know the news, and I don't want your money," answered Jeff contemptuously.

"This is ridiculous," said Mr. Dawkins, regarding him attentively. "Look here, young man: if anything should happen to your employer—I don't say it will, mind, but if it should—you may hear of something to your advantage by calling at this address." He pulled out a card and threw it on the table. "What luck Holt has!" he murmured as he left the room. "But where on earth could he have ever met with such a boy?"

Just before one o'clock, Jeff the Incorruptible had another visitor. A commissionaire called with a note for "Geoffrey Derwent, Esq." *Immediate; Bearer waits,* was underlined upon the envelope.

"Are you Mr. Derwent?" inquired the messenger scrutinisingly; "because I was to give this into your own hands."

"It is all right, my man. Are you from Islington?"

Jeff was afraid there might be bad news from Brown Street, where he called every night and morning.

But the handwriting of the letter, which consisted of but a few words, was strange to him: "A friend wishes to see you at once upon important business at the Bold Templar's Coffee-house, Ludgate Hill. Please keep this communication private. Ask for Mr. Phelps."

When · Jeff looked up, the messenger had vanished.

This young gentleman was not of a romantic turn of mind. "I believe it's Sanders, who wishes to keep me under lock and key till I shall have produced a three-volume novel," mused he. "In that case I shall be a prisoner for life. Or perhaps it's a dodge to get into the office." This last idea seemed probable enough; and before Jeff left, he gave the policeman a hint to look after the premises in his absence, since the boy in charge was but an inefficient guard. It was his own time for dinner, so he had no compunctions about spending some portion of his usual hour in answering the mysterious summons, which considerably excited

his curiosity.   There was a teetotal smack about
the Bold Templar's Coffee-house; but none of Jeff's
acquaintances were teetotalers, having most of them
the power of imbibing spirituous, or at least
malt liquors, without getting hopelessly intoxicated.   Perhaps, after all, the whole thing was a
hoax, to which species of humour the young
gentlemen of the Stock Exchange are almost as
much given as their seniors.   At all events, Jeff
was resolved to see it out.   As he passed by
Lloyd's, two men pushed by him talking eagerly,
and he thought he heard one of them mention the
Flamborough Head.   Was it humanly possible that
that vessel had come safe to port, after so many
weeks and months?   His reason told him it was
not; and yet the incident, taken into connection
with Holt's summons to Liverpool and Mr. Dawkins' hint about great news, was curious.   The
Bold Templar's Coffee - house was a third - rate
establishment, situated, not in the main thoroughfare of Ludgate Hill, but in one of the small streets
to the south of it.   So unpromising, indeed, was
its appearance, that had it been evening instead
of noonday, Jeff might have hesitated to enter
it on such an invitation as he had received.   But
as it was, he walked in unconcernedly enough, and

inquired of a very dirty waiter, who was lounging in the passage, with a napkin under his arm that matched his linen, for Mr. Phelps.

The man nodded, and led the way through a swing-door into a low-roofed and dingy coffee-room, arranged in compartments like tall old-fashioned pews.

" Gent for Mr. Phelps," said the waiter, sharply; and immediately from the farthest corner there emerged a stranger, and came forward to meet the visitor.

A stranger, as I have written, he was to Geoffrey Derwent, and yet there was something about the man not wholly unfamiliar to him. His face was dark and wrinkled, and his hair was gray; but his eyes were bright and piercing. He had never seen so old a face with eyes so young before, save once.

" It was good of you to come so soon, Mr. Derwent, and on so unceremonious a summons," said he, in grave tones. " Oblige me by sitting down for a few minutes, and hearing what I have to say."

He pointed to a seat in the compartment next to that from which he had risen, and lighted better than most by a dusty window.

Then Jeff could see that the man was curiously clothed, like one who had just come from travel in foreign lands, and to whom either time or means had been wanting to equip himself like other people. The latter was probably the case in this instance, for even such clothes as he had were worn and threadbare, as well as being of too slight a texture for the season.

Jeff gazed at him long and earnestly; while his new acquaintance, as though to give the opportunity of doing so, drew out a note-book and cut a pencil.

"We have met before, I believe, Mr. Derwent?" said he, presently, as if in reply to this examination.

"Never. But you bear a strong resemblance to one very dear to me, though you are an older man."

"You mean John Dalton?"

"Yes."

"I am his half-brother, Philip Astor," returned the other, still more gravely than before; "and it is of John Dalton that I wish to speak with you.".

"Have you any news of him, sir?" inquired Jeff, eagerly. "Your tone gives me little hope; and yet there is a report—or at least some sort of talk—in the City that the *Flamborough Head* has come into port."

"Indeed!" returned the other with some surprise. "I am sorry to say, however, the news is false. You are acquainted, I believe, not only with my half-brother, but with his family. Be so kind as to speak out, as I am a little deaf."

"I am well acquainted with them," answered Jeff, in distinct tones; "they are the dearest friends I have in the world."

"And yet they are in bad circumstances, I understand?"

"They are not rich. When one says 'dear,' one does not always mean a money value," returned Jeff, coldly. He began to dislike this man, with whom, too, he now remembered Mr. Dalton had had some sort of quarrel or litigation.

"The object of my inquiries is a friendly one, I do assure you," observed the other, reading his thoughts. "I wish to be assured of our friends' welfare, that is all." He paused; then, with a slight tremor in his voice, continued : "Are they all well?"

"Kitty is well."

"And still Miss Kitty, I suppose?" put in the other, quickly.

"Certainly," returned Jeff, with heightened colour.

"And she is not engaged to anyone that you are aware of? Well, well, I only asked, meaning no offence. And how are the rest of them?"

"Jenny has been very ill, but she is getting somewhat better. She was always delicate, as you are probably aware; and her poor mother's death——"

"I know, I know," interrupted the other, hastily; "that sad news has already reached me."

A heavy sigh broke forth from somewhere in the darkness of the room.

"What is that? We are not alone," said Jeff, angrily. "I do not choose to speak thus of the affairs of others in the presence of strangers."

"It is a friend of mine in the next box."

"I don't care who it is. I won't——" Here Jeff stopped short, transfixed with awe.

A face was looking down upon him over the next partition which he had never thought to see again. It was a worn and weary face, older by ten years than when he had seen it last—as old as that of his present companion, senior (as Jeff knew) to him by many, many years—but it was that of John Dalton.

"Jeff, do you know me?" said a weak and half-choked voice, very different from those musical tones that had once won every ear.

"Oh yes, Mr. Dalton. God be thanked! What joy, what happiness, you will have brought with you!"

"Do you think so?" inquired the other, eagerly, as they pressed each other's hands. "Have they forgiven me, and not yet forgotten me—my dear ones?"

"Sir, they think of you and pray for you—I know Kitty prays for your return even yet—every day and night."

"My Kitty, my own bright Kitty! Jenny, you say, is better. And the boy—dear Tony?"

"He is as blithe as June, sir, and as gentle. To see him watching by his little brother, amusing him——"

"Ay, there is another," said Dalton, gloomily. "Her baby boy."

"And as jolly a little baby as one would wish to see," interposed Jeff, cheerfully. "He is the plaything of the whole house, though Kitty and he are inseparables. They are all well, Mr. Dalton, and need only to see their father's face again to be all happy."

"God bless you, Jeff, for saying so ! I did not dare to ask about them myself, but got Philip here to be my spokesman. Where are they all ? "

"At Mrs. Haywood's, in Brown Street. The old dame is delighted to have them, and they feel quite at home."

"Perhaps there is not much temptation to leave it," observed Dalton, significantly. "Are their friends kind ? "

"Oh yes. There is Dr. Curzon—he came up expressly to see Jenny; and, and—— Why, who could help being kind to them ? "

"I see one who could not help it; but I should like to hear of others. Tell me the truth, Jeff. Are my children quite deserted ? Do none of all my old acquaintances visit the motherless and the poor in their affliction, for my sake or their own ? "

"Well, you see, Jenny has been ill of late——"

"Was it infectious, then ? " inquired the other, apprehensively.

"No, it was not infectious; but when there is illness, it is well to keep a house quiet; and, besides, Kitty made up her mind, when she found herself in charge of the family, and there was a necessity for great economy, to seclude herself as much as possible."

"In spite of invitations and hospitalities," said Dalton, bitterly. "I see. The Riverside people, however, have surely not forsaken them?"

"There was a misunderstanding with Mrs. Campden, sir. Jenny returned some money that she had sent them or lent them; and there has been a breach."

"And 'Uncle George' took his wife's part?"

"Upon my life, sir," said Jeff earnestly, "I don't think he could help it."

"He must have some good in him, since *you* stick by him, Jeff," answered Dalton with a faint smile. "You see how it is, Philip. There are just three—Dr. Curzon, Mrs. Haywood, and this one here. Just three. Think of it!"

"And a very good average," returned Astor curtly. "I have got *one* friend, just one. And perhaps I shall not have him long," added he moodily.

"As long as he lives, Philip," returned Dalton, quietly taking the other's hand. "Jeff, you have stood by me, and mine. Take my brother also into your wide and loving heart. It is through him next to God, that I am now alive. It is through him that those who, I have just heard you say— and bless you for it—were dearest to you, are

about to be made happy. I cannot see them to-
day—at least not yet. I have something to do
first; something "—here his voice grew very harsh
and stern—" that has nothing to do with happiness,
but with woe, and wrath, and retribution. You
are in Richard Holt's employment, it seems, as
good men have been before you. Where is he?"

"He left his office this morning, he said for
Plymouth, but as I have reason to believe, for
Liverpool."

Dalton and Astor exchanged significant glances.

"Ill news flies apace," said the latter. "What
matters it? He cannot escape us."

"That is true," answered Dalton, in a slow tone
of satisfaction. "He would have to take my life
ere he could do that."

"And mine, John," observed Philip in a tone of
reproach.

"I know it," returned Dalton with tender
gravity; "but you and I are one, brother."

CHAPTER XII.

WHEN Dalton arrived at Liverpool upon the day of his leaving Riverside, it was too late to go on board the *Flamborough Head,* and therefore, notwithstanding his desire to be economical, he was compelled to sleep at an hotel. The next morning was a wet one; yet, for the sake of a few shillings, he sent his luggage by a porter's truck, and went down through the rain to the docks on foot. It was just such an arrangement of the "penny-wise and pound foolish" sort as those unaccustomed to frugality are wont to make; and grievously did he afterwards repent of it. He found everything on board in confusion; there was a difficulty, or seemed one, about getting at the contents of his portmanteau; his cabin indeed was infinitely better than he had expected, thanks to his wife's kind extravagance, and not a moment was to be lost in

acknowledging *that*. One thing and the other, in
short, combined to make him careless of so small a
matter as damp raiment, and the end of it all was
rheumatism in the knees. This is a malady—let
those who enjoy the acquaintance of sciatica boast
as they please—not easily matched for habitual
discomfort, and it crippled Dalton. It was some
time before he could leave his cabin and so much
as crawl about the saloon, and even then he was
subject to severe relapses. On one of his " better
days" he managed to make the grand tour of the
vessel; he was on that part of the deck appro-
priated to second-class passengers, when suddenly
his pains came on, and he fell rather than sat down
upon a coil of rope.

"You are ill, Mr. Dalton; shall I give you an
arm?" said someone in cold but courteous tones;
and, looking up, he saw his half-brother.

The phrase "More familiar than welcome,"
which would have suited with the sight of Astor's
face a few days back, had now no meaning for
Dalton. Any face that he had known of old, and
which therefore reminded him of home, was welcome
to him.

"What! you here, Philip?" said he, with genuine
emotion. A pleased expression flitted across the

other's grave gray features; for hitherto his half-brother had been scrupulous to call him "Mr. Astor."

"Yes, John, it is I. I suppose I must say I am sorry to see you, since you are outward bound, like myself, but, unlike me, have left so many dear ones behind you. You are in pain, I fear, too?"

"I have got a touch of rheumatism; that is all. But how came *you* here? I thought, from what Holt told me, you had left England some time ago."

"It is not well to believe what Richard Holt tells you about anything," answered the other bitterly. "I should have thought you had found out that for yourself by this time. If otherwise, I am surprised you speak to me, after what he must needs have told you about me."

"He told me nothing, except that he was dissatisfied with you; by which I understood that you had parted company on account of some business disagreement."

"Dissatisfied?" echoed Astor, contemptuously. "Yes, he has cause to be dissatisfied with me: he took me into his employment upon speculation— in the hope that, after all, I should make good my claim of legitimacy against yourself. He didn't tell you *that*, I'll warrant."

"No, indeed," said Dalton. "On the contrary, he gave me to understand—though he never actually said so—that he retained you out of his regard for me."

"Regard for *you!*" exclaimed Astor, with a bitter laugh. "Why, he would have put all your money into my pocket—minus what he claimed as his own share—if the thing could have been done. I would have gained from you what I considered my own, Mr. Dalton—as I still consider it—but I would never have played you false, as *he* did."

"But you have quarrelled with him, you confess yourself?" remarked the other, cautiously. He had his own suspicions of his late business friend, but he felt that that was no reason for believing all that a personal enemy might say against him.

"Yes, we have quarrelled," answered Astor frankly; "and, legally, it is I who have been in the wrong. He led me to imagine that I was his partner. The whole plot is plain to me now; but I was deceived as easily as a child by a trick at cards. John, tell me the truth. Did that villain ever hint to you that I had forged his name?"

"Never, upon my honour, Philip: he would not have dared to do it."

"I thank you, brother, for that word," answered

Astor, gravely. "Well, he might have done it, and, in a sort of way, yet spoken what was true. He knew that I had meant no wrong, but it might have been hard to persuade others so. He gained a hold on me, at all events; and when I got to know more of his affairs than was agreeable to him, he used his hold. I am no felon, John, believe me; and yet, thanks to Richard Holt, I am transported. He has compelled me to leave England—as he has compelled *you*."

"He has not compelled *me*," answered Dalton, haughtily. "In fact, I am doing so contrary to his advice."

"I understand," said Astor, quietly. "He wanted you to part with your shares; but your motto was, 'Stick to the *Lara*.'"

"Good heavens! how do you know that? Why —Philip—it was you who wrote that warning letter?" exclaimed Dalton, in astonishment.

"If four words can be said to be a letter; yes, I did. You are bound for Brazil, to discover if the advice be good, for yourself. Time will show; yet, I think, you have acted wisely."

"But, Philip, why should you have done so? Why should you have taken the trouble to do so good a turn to one whose interests—and unhappily

whose acts, though of necessity—have been so
antagonistic to your own?"

"Well, there was a reason; for which you yourself owe me no thanks."

"I owe you thanks, whatever it was."

"No. The thanks, if they turn out to be owed
to anyone, are due to Kitty."

"To my daughter Kitty?"

"Yes; and my *niece*," answered the other.
"Listen, John. Years ago, when that unhappy
litigation between us had resulted—though, as *I*
thought, and as Holt thought, only temporarily—
in my defeat, I set foot for the first time under
your roof. We met; not cordially, but without ill
blood; and you would have behaved, if I had permitted you to do so, with what you doubtless considered—and indeed what was so, from your point
of view—with generosity. Well, we need not talk
of that now. You refused to acknowledge me as
your brother. As I left your house, full of wrath
and bitterness, a little maiden, beautiful as a fairy,
ran up to me in the hall, and with eager eyes
exclaimed: 'Why, you are Uncle Philip!' I
snatched her up in my arms and kissed her. It
was very illogical in me, no doubt—for if the little
lady had known the circumstances of the case, she

would probably have been the last to give me such a title—but I loved her for acknowledging the relationship that you denied. She has forgotten me, no doubt, but I never forgot her; and when, years afterwards, I discovered—no matter how—that my employer, Holt, was bent on making her his wife——"

"Ah, you know that too, do you? I have sometimes suspected it," said Dalton gloomily. "Go on."

"Well, I say, when I found that that false hound had dared to lift his eyes to Kitty, I swear I hated him for that worse than all the rest. I had no means of foiling him, of course; but I felt that his opportunity could only lie in your necessity, and therefore strove to avert your ruin. What losses he has caused you, I know not; my belief is he made a catspaw of you from the first, and has robbed you right and left; but with the *Lara* he has still connection, that is certain. I heard from Brand (himself dismissed like me for knowing too much) that Holt was pressing you to sell your shares, and so I wrote to you to stick to them. That's the whole story."

Much of this was, of course, news to Dalton, though somehow it only tended to confirm his own suspicions. Yet, after all, like them it was but vague. He had a greater distrust of Holt than ever, yet he had no more tangible ground than before for entertaining it. Had the opportunity, for example, been at once afforded him of returning to England and taxing his late business friend with mal-practices, he would scarcely have taken advantage of it. No proof of any kind was to his hand. As time went on, however, and he got to know more of his half-brother, his confidence in him increased, and in proportion his suspicions of the man he had got by that time to consider their common enemy. The little episode of Kitty's reception of her uncle touched her father's heart, and out of it there flowed a tenderness not only towards Kitty herself, but towards him who had thus recalled her and spoken of her so fondly; while the anger Astor felt against Holt for daring to wish to win Kitty's favour, combining with his own suspicions of that intention, made somehow a still stronger bond between them.

The intimacy between the saloon passenger and the second-class man, as well as the unmistakable family likeness between them, excited considerable curiosity and some comment; and here again Dalton endeared himself to Philip by at once owning

him as his half-brother, without saying a word
of his illegitimacy. John's mother was supposed
to have been married again to a person of larger
means than her first husband, and hence the difference of the social position of the two brothers.
It was generous of him, for it cost some sacrifice
of pride, but Philip was more than grateful for it.
No liberality which John had shown him in the
past touched him half as nearly. Unhappily, he
was in no position to repay him; for he was going
to Brazil a mere adventurer, as friendless, and even
more penniless than his kinsman; but as a comforter and, when occasion required, as a sick nurse,
his companionship was invaluable. The two men
would sit together for hours talking over Holt's
conduct, chiefly in relation to John; speculating as
to whether he had played him false in this and that
affair, but especially concerning the mine. And
then for relief they would turn to Kitty, of whom
Philip was never tired of hearing; and from her
John would diverge to his wife and the other
children, and find at least a patient and apparently
an interested listener.

It was curious how the adversity which thus
knit John to Philip isolated him from the rest of
his fellow-creatures. His genial nature had been

nipped and frozen by its cold breath, and where the blossoms of wit and fancy had been wont to hang in such profusion, there was naught now but bare boughs. If to any one among the saloon passengers on board the *Flamborough Head* the social reputation of John Dalton was known by repute, he must needs have thought it ill earned. Dalton was, to be sure, an invalid ; but even when he was able to take his seat at table, or hobble up to smoke a cigar upon the deck, he did not mingle in the conversation, but sat in silence and sad thought. He was polite, of course, and answered when addressed ; but that was all. There were some young ladies on board who interested him—by some faint resemblance perhaps to Kitty or Jenny ; but he was constantly asking himself how it was with Edith and the little household at Sanbeck. The recollection of the unpaid premium to the *Palm Branch* also occurred to him, and gave him great uneasiness ; for though he strove to believe that Mr. Campden would surely discharge that debt for him, his thoughts were full of bitterness and disbelief in the loyalty of all friends. From the little gaieties and . amusements of life on shipboard he shrank with pain except on one occasion. The pretty custom had just come in vogue of committing a miniature vessel, decked with ribbons, and named after some young-lady passenger—to mid-ocean, laden with letters for England, in hopes that some homeward-bound ship would pick it up and act as postman. In this case, the fairy craft happened to be named the *Edith*; and since it could but carry a very limited mail-bag, there was much competition for the privilege of sending letters by it. The coincidence of the name with that of his wife made John strangely solicitous to be one of the favoured few, and he succeeded in his desire. Perhaps his only happy hour on board the *Flamborough Head* was during the launching of this fragile toy; his eyes were the last to watch it as it rose and fell upon the calm bosom of the ocean in their wake. After that day there was no more calm. Stormy weather set in, and with it the pangs of his rheumatism increased. He was confined to his berth, and day and night lay listening to the roar of wind and wave. Philip came to him, and sat by his side, conversing as long as it was possible to converse; but after a time the gale so increased that no human voice could well be heard.

One day—it was but noon, but the cabin window was so hidden by sheets of water that it was almost dark—John asked with difficulty, "Is there danger, Philip?"

His brother nodded gravely, holding on meanwhile to the side of the berth. The ship so pitched and lurched that the floor was as often the ceiling as the floor; the howling of the wind and the roar of the sea were deafening and incessant; but above them both could be heard hurried movements upon the deck.

"They are getting out the boats. Is it not so, Philip?"

"I will go and see. Do not fear, brother; I will not desert you."

"I fear nothing—only for my poor wife and the children; thank God, I am well within the days of grace, however." John Dalton's thoughts amid that whirl and woe were centred on the premium of his life assurance. Presently the door was burst open—it would open in no other way now—and Philip rushed in.

"Quick, quick! You must get up; and I will carry you on deck."

"Not I," answered Dalton resolutely. "What should I do, a poor cripple, in this tumult? Could I jump into a boat? Could I live in one, if I did? No. Let me drown in peace."

Philip's only answer was to seize him in his powerful arms and drag him from his berth.

From thence, by immense exertion, he got him

across the saloon; but up the cabin stairs, now steep, now sloping, and now staggering towards them like a thing of life, it was impossible to carry him: he was not only a helpless cripple, but every movement gave him torture.

"Leave me, Philip, leave me!" exclaimed he vehemently. "God will reward you, though He will not suffer you to save me. Tell Edith my last breath was——"

There was a rush of water down the cabin stairs that swept the men apart, and dashed the speaker senseless against the cabin wall.

When he came to himself, he was lying on the floor wet through; the turmoil of the elements had nowise abated, but the trampling and hurrying overhead had ceased. Sometimes all was in darkness—when the maimed and shattered vessel fell into the trough of the sea—and sometimes there was light enough to behold the devastation and wreck of the saloon as the ship battled to the surface, and was hurried on the crest of a wave. From her aimless and uncertain progress, it was evident that she no longer obeyed the helm, but was rolling like a log, now under, and now above the water.

If John's personal discomfort had been less, he

might even now have congratulated himself that he had lived his life thus long, and had not ended it upon Bleabarrow Crags, as he had once thought to do: Edith could now have no sort of difficulty in realising the five thousand pounds from the *Palm Branch*, and there would be no guilt of self-murder upon his soul. But his knees gave him such intolerable pain that he could think of little else. He contrived, however, to drag himself on to one of the couches let into the sides of the saloon, and presently swooned away there.

When Dalton next woke to life he was in his own berth; the roar of the tempest had greatly diminished, but there was a slush and whirl of water in his ears; and he perceived—or was he dreaming?—that some articles in his cabin were advancing to and retreating from him in the strangest manner: they were in fact afloat. From the complete absence of any sound save that of the elements, it was plain to Dalton that the ship was deserted. Yet how, if this were so, could he have been conveyed back to his berth? His pains had abated, but he was faint and sick with hunger, and conscious of some strange disturbance in his brain. Was it a dream, or was it the fact, that some one was splashing about the cabin? Dr. Curzon, perhaps, upon his pony : yes, and with a prescription too, which he persisted in thrusting into his mouth—a mixture of biscuit and brandy, which so revived him, that he presently sat up, and said : " Hollo, Philip ! "

" Hollo, old fellow," answered his half-brother cheerily ; " the old ship floats, you see, still."

" Yes ; only the water is inside of her as well as outside of her; is it not ?" said Dalton. It was a point that puzzled him, and which he really wished to have cleared up ; but the other mistook it for a joke.

" Come, that is spoken like yourself, John. You are getting round now, though you have had a bad touch of it."

Then Dalton began dimly to comprehend that he had been ill for days.

" Where is everybody, Philip ?" inquired he suddenly.

" The ship is water-logged : as for the people, I don't know for certain," answered Philip gravely ; " but I fear that you and I are all that now remain of them. That day when· you saw me last—to know me—was one I shall never forget. The scene on deck was heart-rending. The women—— You remember those two girls who launched the *Edith ?*"

John nodded : he remembered their doing *that.*

"Well, they clung about the captain like poor demented creatures at the feet of their idol. Their shrieks, their cries for help, where no help could come, while the wind and waves stormed at them like devils, were terrible to listen to. The launching of the boats was with great difficulty effected; but some were staved in, and some were swamped with all on board, before our eyes. It was a sea, the captain said, such as it was scarce possible for a boat to live in. I told him how you were left below stairs; but he said, taking into account your maimed condition, you had as good a chance of life —if chance there was—in remaining there, as in endeavouring to leave the ship."

"And *you?*" inquired Dalton, taking the other's hand and pressing it with what little strength he had.

"Well, [I thought I would see the thing out along with you, John. The boats I verily believe are lost, with all that went with them; and the old ship herself was bound to have gone down too, but for some empty casks it seems she has below."

"There is hope in your eyes, Philip!" cried the other eagerly. "Is a sail in sight?"

"No, indeed. Only, since the ship has floated

so long, lop-sided and water-logged though she be——"

" There is land ahead ?" exclaimed Dalton excitedly.

" You have hit it, John. There is land of some sort; and you must make shift to come on deck and look at it."

CHAPTER XIII.

" To come on deck and look at it " is not quite the professional phrase for sighting land and deciding upon its bearings. But the fact was that, *except* Dalton, there had probably not been a man on board the *Flamborough Head* who knew less about nautical matters than Philip Astor. These two men were, in fact, the very last that a ship's captain would have selected to help him to navigate a vessel, and almost the last whom any one would have chosen as coadjutors in such an adventure as lay before them. Dalton was a product of the highest civilisation, if not of culture. His natural place was in drawing-rooms and club-houses; he had never done anything of a menial, or indeed a useful kind since he had been a fag at Eton, and was "blown up" (and worse), like another King Alfred, for burning his master's toast. The idea of his being shipwrecked on a desolate island was preposterous, and should have placed the stern Fate that brought him there among the first class of humorists.

Philip Astor had, it is true, been more knocked about in the world, but the shifts and contrivances to which he had been pushed had been those of town life; he knew scarcely more of what may be called the rudiments of life—how to build, to cook, to clothe himself, even to guess the time by the position of the sun—than his more highly-placed half-brother. At present, however, he had much the advantage over him in health and vigour; and he now put forth his strength to the uttermost to carry his companion through the slush of the saloon, and to assist him up the now sidelong staircase to the deck.

Dalton was better, however; he got along with much less difficulty than he had expected, and the fresh air revived him wonderfully. The prospect itself was not exhilarating. The storm had ceased, but left the sea of a dull leaden colour, as though its liver (as must certainly have been the case if it had one) had been much "upset." The ship it was a compliment to call a ship at all. The masts were gone, though the stumps were left, and one of the steam-funnels; some broken rigging was trailing in the water, which was level with the bulwarks on one side, while the other was lifted up, and to a landsman's eye threatened an overturn every moment. To stand upon the sloping deck without holding on to some fixed object was impossible. Still the vessel moved, though very slowly, and fortunately in the direction favourable to the voyagers' hopes.

In front of them lay a low, scantily-wooded island, with sandy shore, and to this they were tending, though not in a straight course. The wind was slight, and from the north-east, and bore them towards a rocky promontory to the south of the island, which formed one side of a little bay. If the ship should drive ashore inside this promontory, matters might go well; but if outside, there was the open sea again, where the question of her remaining afloat could be only one of a few hours at farthest. The helm, even if she had a rudder— which was more than doubtful—was gone, and the two men watched the course of the vessel in utter helplessness.

Suddenly the wind shifted a little, and turned her head more to the south-east; that is, to seaward. It was now obvious that she was about to miss the promontory. The two men looked at one another in silent despair.

Then suddenly Dalton cried: "Can you find a hatchet, Philip?"

Fortunately, in a corner of the deck there was one—the last left of many that had been used to cut away the ship's gear on that terrible day.

"If we can get rid of that rigging, perhaps she will wear a bit."

A few powerful strokes from Philip's arm freed the ship from this encumbrance, and at once she rose a little in the water, and altered her course as was desired.

It was not just then a time for compliments, but afterwards Philip told John that from that moment he was reconciled to the idea of his (John's) having succeeded to the Dalton property; for that a man with such intelligence deserved to be the head of the family. Thus the dismasted ship, though rolling and swaying, yet floated into what, by comparison with where she had been, might be called port; that is to say, under the sheltered side of the promontory, close to which, and in almost shallow water, she grounded upon the sand, as safe (while the weather continued fine) as though she were in the London Docks.

Of this much in respect of their common adventures both John and Philip often spoke; but with regard to their subsequent life upon the spot they had thus had the good fortune to reach, these twin Crusoes were very reticent. The fact was that from their excessive ignorance, they got on worse than almost any persons in such a situation could have been expected to do. The island, a small one, lying to the south of the West India group, and little else than barren rock, could certainly not have sustained them had they been dependent upon the development or even the realisation of its resources. But fortunately for them, the sea had not robbed the *Flamborough Head* of its contents, although it had damaged much of them excessively. They lost no time in removing all the stores they could lay their hands on to land, and took up their abode in a cave upon the promontory, on which they erected a flag, to call the attention of any passing ship. They had to thank the island for nothing save indeed for a limpid spring, without which it might have gone hard with them, neither of them possessing that kind of genius that hits upon scientific plans of extracting fresh water from plants, precious stones, or even from salt water.

Before they got to the end of their preserved

meats and vegetables, their "extracts" of this and
that, and their ship biscuits, a Spanish vessel, bound
for Rio, passed by, and, seeing their signal, sent
a boat, and brought them off. They came away in
very good case, and almost fit to be Fellows of All
Souls, *bene nati* (though one of them, it is true, the
law held to be illegitimate), *bene vestiti* (for they had
had all their fellow-passengers' clothes to choose
from, besides their own); *et mediocriter docti*, that is
to say, they were almost as ignorant of how to provide for themselves as when they landed. Yet they
had learned something : to respect one another very
heartily, and also—this was especially the case with
John—to look upon life otherwise than through the
tinted spectacles of society. He had had cause to
recognise very literally "a man and a brother" in
his unacknowledged kinsman, to whom he owed
his life twice and thrice over. If Philip had not
remained with him on board ship, he would have
perished in his narrow cabin, or certainly have
never reached land; and if he had reached land,
he would have perished there, but for Philip's
companionship, cheerfulness and sympathy. Even
as it was, he had been consumed with apprehensions about those dear ones he had left at Sanbeck,
and only too truly, as we know, had his heart mis-

given him respecting Edith, overwhelmed as she must needs be by this time with the news of the loss of the *Flamborough Head.* His dead wife, his orphaned children, were spectacles that were rarely absent from his eyes, and he had needed all Philip's sanguine arguments and pleasant prophecies to win him from despondency. For the rest, his out-of-door life and simple fare had physically bettered him; he had got rid of his lameness, and felt himself strong enough for any hardships that might yet lie before him in his quest. Upon visiting San José, and seeing with his own eyes how matters were with the gold mine, his mind was as fixed as ever: much as he yearned for home, he was resolved not to return thither with the mission unaccomplished for which he had left it; and the opportunity was now—at last—afforded him of effecting his object. The two castaways had a sufficient stock remaining of the good things saved from the *Flamborough Head* to make them very welcome on board the *Cadiz* without the payment of passage-money; so Dalton's slender purse was still intact upon their arrival at Rio.

Here, however, misfortune was awaiting him; a letter that had long been lying for him at the post-office informed him of his wife's death. His forebodings, as we know, had pointed that way with an inexorable finger, but they had not prepared him for it, and for a time the news utterly overwhelmed him. To say that Edith had been his better-half, his *alter ego*, and the good angel of his life, so far as he had permitted her to be so, was feebly indeed to express what she had been to him; and with his anguish there was mingled the most bitter remorse; for had he not killed her with the work of his own hands? Out of the very depths of his wretchedness, however, came a motive for action; all the reparation he could now make to his lost love and lover was to further the interests of her children. Whether they were still left to him, or in what plight, he could not tell, nor had he the means of informing them that they had yet a father, since, unhappily, the mail-boat had left Rio the very day before his arrival.

There was time to reach San José and return before the next steamer left the port for England; so the two brothers at once started for their destination. They had to husband their resources, and travelled slowly, and with what, six months ago, Dalton would have felt to be great discomfort, much increased by their ignorance of Spanish, or of the native tongue. And even when they reached

San José, they found they had by no means accomplished their journey. The *Lara* mine, about which people seemed to know little or nothing, was still far away, and since it lay out of the main track, they were compelled to push on thither on foot.

The scenery was splendid. They were always in sight of the stupendous Cordilleras, although they scarcely seemed to approach them nearer. The gold district lay between them and these mountains. In the good old times, the precious metal had been exclusively the produce of alluvial washings; but these had long become exhausted, and the gold now yielded was dug deep up out of the solid rock, which cropped up on the surface in dome-like masses, often covered with foliage. If Dalton's mind had not been bent so earnestly on a single end, he could not but have been enchanted with these scenes, in which men contended so energetically with Nature and yet could not mar her beauties. The two friends had passed by three such mines, and on the third morning of their travels came upon a fourth. They asked its name of one they met upon the road who knew a little English, and he had told them it was called the *Quito*. It was situated in the most beautiful spot they had yet reached.

"Forest on forest" hung above it "like cloud on

cloud," so that, though itself in an elevated region, it looked sunk in a shady vale. A little river ran through it, which turned the stamping-mills and the pumping machinery, which was in full action. The din was incessant, yet by no means deafening; and the bustle and movement, contrasted with the quietness and sublimity of its natural surroundings, were very striking. The chief engineer—who was one Mr. Blake, as usual an Englishman—gave a welcome to his two wandering fellow-countrymen that was more than cordial; there being no inn in the place, he invited them to dine, and after that repast showed them over the works, which were of considerable extent. Not content with watching the tram-carriages, bearing each a ton of the mineral, coming steeply up from the shafts, they descended in them to the depth of nearly a thousand feet to the very home of the gold. Afterwards they had explained to them how the rough rock gives forth its treasure; saw it freed from slate upon the spalling-floors, and afterwards stamped fine, issuing through the copper grates, to pass over the bullock skins, and—lower down the inclined tables—over woollen cloths, the washing of which yields the golden fruitage. Then they once more repaired to Mr. Blake's one-storied dwelling, tiled and slated, with its broad verandah hung with flowers and creepers, to be again refreshed before they started on their way. With pardonable pride he spoke of the *Quito's* prosperity, which, he said, was but of recent date. He had been its engineer but for a few months, and had taken it when it was in a very depressed condition. There had been even a doubt as to whether it would repay working at all, all its ancient wealth having been supposed to be exhausted.

His wife, also English, listened to the story of his achievement as though she had heard no word of it before.

"Your friend has suffered a recent loss, I fear?" observed the engineer apart to Philip, for Dalton was in deep mourning; and the spectacle of the domestic happiness of his host and hostess, and of their prosperity, touched his bruised heart with a sense of contrast.

"Yes," returned Philip; "losses of all kinds. His wife is dead, and his fortune has been spent in the same sort of adventure that has turned out so differently in your case."

"Indeed; I am sorry for it. The fact is, only about one in six of these Brazil mines, formerly so profitable, now pay their expenses. There is also a deal of roguery about some of them, very difficult for those who are not upon the spot—I mean for English shareholders—to get to the bottom of. I am afraid some of my own calling—who are my fellow-countrymen, like yourselves—do not always keep their hands clean. The agents, the experts, and the engineers, have it all their own way, you see, out here."

"Just so. Well, we are now bound for my friend's mine; just such a one as you have described, I fear; the *Lara,* and if you can tell us anything about it, he will be greatly indebted to you."

"The *Lara!*" echoed the engineer. "Are you really serious? Did you come from England to look after the *Lara?*"

"Yes; though, I am afraid, upon a fool's errand. The people at Rio and those we have met upon the road seemed to know little or nothing about it?"

"Are you talking about the *Lara?*" here put in Dalton, earnestly. "Can our host tell us anything about it, Philip? Pray, don't fear to tell me the worst, Mr. Blake," added he, addressing his host.

"I don't know what you mean by 'the worst,'

Mr. Dalton," returned the engineer, curtly ; " but I
have only to say that this mine here *is* the *Lara*.
It has only been called the *Quito* for the last six
months."

CHAPTER XIV.

Mr. Blake's astounding announcement was of course a revelation to his two guests, but they had the prudence to conceal the fact as best they could. The engineer was a thoroughly honourable fellow, and consequently loyal to his employers. It would have been difficult to convince him—and on the whole Dalton thought it better not to try—that the mine with the conduct of which he had been entrusted—and here again Holt had shown his peculiar idiosyncrasy in favour of honesty in other people—was in fact a swindle of the most Machiavelian kind. Instead of existing on paper only, like other fraudulent institutions of a similar class, it did *not* exist on paper—that is, under its real name—at all, but had a very actual and *bonâ fide* existence in fact. The last local agent of the *Lara*, Brooks, had been in the pay of Holt, and had played into the hands

of his creature Tobbit, the expert, in representing
the mine to the English shareholders as worked out
and valueless.   The whole affair had been transacted with consummate skill, but not, as we have
seen, without exciting the suspicions of Philip
Astor, and even of a certain financial circle in the
City with which Sir Richard Beevor and Mr. Binks
were connected.   Up to this time, however, the real
state of things was undiscovered, and for the present, Dalton thought it better it should remain so.
Of the proofs of it he presently acquired full possession, but in dealing with so astute a scoundrel
as Holt it was expedient to be very cautious; while
so long as the latter was kept in ignorance of Philip
and himself having been saved from the *Flamborough Head*, they would have a great advantage
over him.

Dalton therefore confined the statement of his
wrongs to the fact, that endeavours had been made
to persuade him to part with certain shares in the
Lara, as being of no value. His account of the
affair was not indeed very intelligible; and Philip
had to lend assistance by hinting that his brother's
grievance had—as grievances are apt to do—not
left him altogether a logical being upon this particular topic; but the pair so far succeeded, that

when they quitted Mr. Blake's hospitable roof, that gentleman had no suspicion that he had been entertaining an angel unawares in the person of one of his proprietors; while, on the other hand, it was pretty evident to Dalton that the only individual who held any shares in the *Lara* beside himself was in truth Richard Holt, who held half of them, and had certainly left no stone unturned to secure the other moiety; while in the meantime, as though already possessed of it, he had been receiving the proceeds of the whole, which made up a very substantial income.

"But for your '*Stick to the Lara*,' Philip," said John with grateful frankness, "I believe I should have let the scoundrel buy my shares of me for a song."

"Nay, brother, it was not much to do—the writing those four words; but I hope you will stick to *me*, in recollection of them," answered Philip. The words were said in jest, but the tone had a serious sadness in it, which stung the other to the quick.

"Do you doubt it, Philip?" said he. "Do you conceive it possible, that when I have grown rich again—'assumed my former social position,' as Mrs. Campden called it (I wonder how that woman is behaving to my poor children; however, George will keep her straight), that I shall inherit with it my former follies; that I shall not know my true friends, those who have been tried in the fire —and the water—from the false ones, and above all, shall not cleave to the brother to whom I shall owe all?"

"We shall be quits," said Astor, pressing his hand, "and more than quits, when you introduce me to Kitty as 'Uncle Philip.'"

"Then I hope we shall be quits within the next six weeks," was John's reply.

They returned to Rio, however, only just in time to catch the steamer *Sancho*, the fore-cabin fare of which almost exhausted their finances. The ship was a slow one compared with the *Flamborough Head*, and Dalton was in such a state of impatience and anxiety throughout the voyage that Philip feared he would have had a fever. A thousand apprehensions consumed him, and as many hopes: among the former was the dread that some news of their having been rescued by the Spanish vessel should somehow reach England before them, and set Holt upon his guard.

From Liverpool they came straight to town, yet not without some vague tidings of passengers having been picked up from the *Flamborough Head* preceding them, as we have seen, to London. So much, indeed, Holt's Liverpool agent had telegraphed to him as took him thither in hot haste to learn the truth. John and Philip had, however, taken the precaution to enter themselves on board the *Sancho* under false names, nor was it likely that they two of all that sailed in the ill-fated steamer should have come home to blast his fortunes.

CHAPTER XV.

JEFF remained at his post in Abdell Court for the remainder of that eventful day, though with a mind but little disposed for his business duties. As he had expected, however, and to his great relief, his employer did not return. The young fellow would have found it difficult indeed to maintain in his presence that indifferent air and manner which Dalton had enjoined upon him; and however successfully he had played an assumed part with the editor of "The Smellfungus Magazine," it is doubtful whether he would have been equally fortunate with Richard Holt. When the office closed he betook himself at once to Brown Street, where he found Jenny, for the first time since her illness, sitting in the little upstairs parlour—to which, even with her ordinary lodgers, Mrs. Haywood hesitated to give the title of drawing-room, but modestly termed it her "first-floor front." There were flowers in the room, and in the window-sill there was a flower-box full of bud and blossom that filled the air with fragrance.

"Is it not beautiful?" cried Jenny, drawing her visitor's attention at once to this unwonted ornament. "Does not our room look a perfect bower?"

"A very proper cage for a sick bird to dwell in, till she is strong enough to fly at large in the sunny south," answered Jeff gallantly.

"Now, none of *that*, Jeff; I am not Mr. Sanders, remember; so please to stick to what *I* know is your proper element—prose. I can't think what has come to dear Kitty, that she should suddenly rush into these extravagances. It is not only flowers, but all sorts of delights and delicacies; and not for my sake only, for she has actually bought Tony a trap, bat, and ball! One would have thought she had had a fortune left her—except for her face, poor darling." Here her voice grew suddenly grave. "I am afraid there is something—I mean, more than Tony and the baby and myself—upon her mind, Jeff. I can't make her out at all. She is sometimes quite extravagantly gay: a put-on manner, I am sure; and then again she becomes more depressed than I have ever yet seen her; and *that*, alas! I can see is natural. Do you know anything, dear Jeff, about my Kitty that I *don't* know?"

Jenny looked at him very earnestly as she said these words, but the young man's face only reflected her own quiet sorrow.

"Nothing, I think, Jenny, that *you* don't know," he answered. "She has avoided me—I may almost say shrunk from me—for this long time; ever since you have been ill, indeed."

"And she has seen Mr. Holt," sighed Jenny. "Oh, why—oh, why have I been struck down like this," added she passionately, "and rendered a useless burden, while all things have been going wrong. Jeff, you'll lose her: mark my words, we shall all lose her, and she will fling herself away upon that man for our poor sakes."

"Don't, Jenny, don't! I beseech you not to give way. Heaven will not permit so terrible a self-sacrifice."

"Ah, you think so," returned Jenny bitterly. "It is a happy faith."

"It is a true one."

"What, that horrible things are not permitted to happen every day? I see there is another mail from Rio : the *Sancho* has arrived. That makes the *fifth* ; and still no news—no gleam of hope."

"There is hope always, Jenny." She looked up at him as quickly as the bird to which he had likened her, with swiftly scrutinising glance.

"He has come ! Our father is alive !"

Then, but for his arm, she would have fallen. Her cheeks were white, her eyes were closed; she lay upon his breast like a thing of stone.

"Great heaven ! have I killed her with my stupid folly ?" exclaimed Jeff in horror. "How could I hope to keep a secret from eyes like hers ! —Jenny, Jenny, speak to me !"

"I hear you : I shall live to see him yet !" she murmured faintly. "Lay me down—with my face to the wall, Jeff. Leave me alone with my Maker, whom I have denied. He will send the tears presently."

"You will not speak of this, Jenny—just yet ?" said he, once more alarmed at her long silence.

"To no human ear : no, Jeff. Leave me now, and go to Kitty."

Jeff left the room, closing the door softly behind him. In the little passage he met Nurse Haywood.

"Well, Miss Jenny is getting on nicely, Master Geoffrey, is she not ?"

" Yes, nurse. But she is tired, and wishes to get a little rest; so do not let her be disturbed. Where is Kitty ?"

" Lor' bless ye; why where should she be except with the baby ! She can scarce ever be got to let him out of her sight. It's my opinion, what with attending to that dear child, and housekeeping, and always being worried about this and that, as she is a-wearing herself out. I daren't tell Miss Jenny, but I have come across Miss Kitty at times when she looks fit to break her heart, though she has always a smile and a kind word for a body when she speaks to one."

" I hope she will speak to *me*, nurse. Please to say I wish to see her on very particular business, and that I will not detain her long."

As he waited in the sitting-room downstairs, revolving in his mind how he should break his great news to Kitty, but failing to hit upon a plan, there re-entered to him Mrs. Haywood.

" Miss Kitty is very sorry, sir, but she is much engaged; and if you would kindly write her a line instead of seeing her——"

" I *must* see her," interrupted Geoffrey impatiently. " Did you not tell her my business was very particular ?"

" Well, yes, Master Jeff, I did; and that was

the very thing, to tell you the honest truth, as seemed to scare her. She has got enough and to spare on her poor mind already, you see."

"Please go and tell her, nurse, that it is absolutely indispensable I should see her, but that what I have to say will not distress her. Be sure you tell her *that.*"

"Lor', Master Jeff, you ain't a got any good news for her, have you?" answered the old lady in a trembling voice. "Nothing about Mr. John—him as I remember as young as you be, and as comely?"

"There is no time to lose about what I have to say," answered Jeff, with as constrained a manner as nature permitted him to assume; "and I do beg you will give my message." His heart smote him at having to snub the good old dame, but he was also irritated at her sagacity, or rather at the transparency of his own attempts to conceal his errand. If his heart had been in literature, Mr. Sanders would have read him as easily as a proof-sheet: it was only where his feelings were not concerned that Geoffrey Derwent could play the hypocrite. While he was still conning that unwonted part, Kitty entered the room.

"Well, Jeff, what is it?" cried she, holding out her hand. "I never knew such a man of mystery. There is baby taking his first beef-tea, and yet

Nurse Haywood says I must leave him to attend
your highness." Her air and manner were too light
and gay to be natural to the occasion in any case;
but contrasted with her looks, which were wan and
worn beyond anything he could have anticipated,
they seemed unreal indeed. Her eyelids were
heavy and swollen, and on her fair white brow
sat unmistakable care and woe.

"I am not come upon my own affairs, dear
Kitty," said Jeff assuringly, "or I would not have
been so importunate."

"The affairs of no one else can interest me—and
all of us—half so much," she answered smilingly.

"I meant to say I should not have intruded
here without a sufficient motive, Kitty—that is all.
The fact is that—that—Mr. Holt——"

At that name a shadow fell on Kitty's face
and chased her smile away; she had been standing hitherto, but now at once sat down.

"That Mr. Holt has had a summons to Liverpool with respect to the arrival of the *Sancho*."

"Ah yes; that is the Rio steamer," she
answered sadly. "The fifth that has brought no
news."

"Well, it *has* brought news."

"Of the *Flamborough Head?* What news?"
inquired Kitty eagerly.

"The ship was wrecked—that's certain; but there were some survivors—two."

"Two," repeated Kitty mournfully; "but two!"

"It is not yet known for certain—that is, publicly—who they are; but—now don't cry, Kitty, *darling* Kitty—but there's a hope."

"A hope? What! of papa's being alive, and he not here! I don't believe it. I want no more such hopes, Jeff; I can't bear them. They are killing me, I tell you; they are driving me to—— I don't know what I am saying, Jeff, but I can't bear them." Her head had fallen forward upon her open hands, and she was crying bitterly.

"Do you suppose I could come here to mock you, Kitty? I came to comfort you, to gladden you."

"To *gladden* me?" She shook her head; her tone was as though he had suggested the most unlikely thing on earth; and yet she raised her face all wet with tears.

"He is alive, Kitty; your father is alive!" She looked like one awakened from a dream; astounded, dazed: the light of joy was breaking on the night of woe, but very slowly.

"Alive! Papa *alive!* Where *is* he?"

In England. You will see him soon. *I* have seen him."

"Thank God, thank God!" she murmured. "Oh, thank God!"

Still she did not rise, nor show any passionate excitement, such as he had expected, and had seen in Jenny. "Is he well, Jeff?" she went on slowly.

"Yes, quite well. Philip Astor is with him, and has been very, very good to him. He is to be called Dalton now, and recognised as his brother."

"When shall I see him? When is he coming? Why is he not here?"

"Because he feared the shock might be too much for you and Jenny. He is close by. Shall I fetch him in, or will you wait a little?"

"Wait a little—just a minute." As she spoke, a joyful cry burst forth in the quiet street. Both glanced through the window, and on the other side of the way was Tony clasped in the arms of a thin grizzled man, in wayworn and outlandish garb. Behind them stood another. They were looking towards the house, and Jeff beckoned to them frantically, and ran to the front door. The next moment, Kitty, sobbing as though her heart would break, was strained passionately to her father's breast.

"Don't cry, don't cry," he whispered, though the tears were falling down his own weather-beaten cheeks like rain; "and you have not yet kissed dear Philip—your Uncle Philip."

CHAPTER XVI.

DOES KITTY KNOW ?

IN Brown Street, Islington, was probably a happier
reunion that evening than any which took place
in more fashionable quarters of the town; yet
it was a happiness tinged with deepest sorrow.
Dalton's return brought with it to his children a
keen sense of the loss of her who would have given
him his fittest welcome; and when his eyes rested
upon his remaining dear ones, he missed his Edith
most.

His first question, after his greetings with Jenny
and the rest were over, was, " Where have they laid
her ? " and he felt pained and sorrowful when he
learned that it was at Sanbeck, hundreds of miles
away; whereas, had it been possible, he would have
visited her grave, and wept over it that very night.
They told him too, at his own desire, of her illness
and death : how she died, as it were, for very love

of him, since the shock of his reported death had killed her. He was silent for many moments, sunk, as it seemed, in a stupor of grief, when Kitty stole from the room and brought down the babe—his Edith's precious legacy, and placed it in his arms.

"We four are still left to you, dear papa," said she. She herself had been supported in her affliction by the sense that others were dependent upon *her*, and she hoped it might be the same with him. And so it was, though in a less measure. He presently grew himself again, and began to ask them about this and that.

"I hope the folks at Riverside have been kind to you, my darlings, since you have been all alone?"

"They meant to be kind, I think," said Kate.

"*Meant* to be kind," repeated her father, frowning. "There is no difficulty about expressing kindness. At least Philip here found none, I know, in my case. Is there anything amiss with the Campdens? What have they done, Jenny?"

"Nothing," answered Jenny sententiously.

"We did not like the manner in which Mrs. Campden behaved to us, after mamma's death," explained Kitty: "it was more manner, perhaps, than anything else; but our hearts were sore, and easily hurt."

"Jenny, tell me," said Dalton. "That woman has behaved badly to you. Is it not so?"

"Not only 'that woman,' but the whole family, in my opinion," returned Jenny dryly.

"Surely not Uncle George?"

"Uncle George is nobody at Riverside; if he had been anybody, there is no saying what might have happened; but he is not. It is a wretched story from beginning to end, and they are wretched people."

"If it be so," said Kitty reprovingly, "do not let us talk about them, on a night like this."

"I am sure I never wish to mention their names," answered Jenny.

"But do you mean to say," said Philip, "that these friends of your father's—rolling in wealth, as I understand they are—never held out a helping hand to you, Jenny?"

"My dear uncle, you don't understand the matter; you should get Mrs. Campden to explain it to you, as she was good enough to do to us: 'Rich people have so many calls.'"

"If this is as you say, I will never set foot in that woman's house again," exclaimed Dalton angrily.

"That will be one call the less for her," observed Jeff pleasantly.

"And the Skiptons? Have you seen nothing of them too?" inquired Dalton.

"My dear papa," said Jenny gravely, "you can't expect folks who respect themselves—or who wish their coachman to respect them—to bring their carriage to Brown Street. It is no good asking after our old friends, for, except dear Dr. Curzon, and those now under this roof, we have none."

It was a relief to Kitty that not a word was said about Mr. Holt, though of him it could certainly not be averred that he had deserted them. To her, terrible as it might seem, and did seem to her own mind, the return of her father was not an unmitigated joy. When Jeff had informed her of it, she had not evinced the delight he had expected, because the thought had flashed upon her, that so far as she was concerned, he had returned too late. She was not indeed pledged to Holt, but she felt compromised as respected him, and in honour bound to accept him as her future husband. For some days past her mind had been made up for the sacrifice, and she had already plunged into little expenses upon Jenny's account in anticipation of it. The money that was to take her sister to the sea, and bring back the roses to her cheek, and which Holt had offered, she had resolved not to decline. She was already under a pecuniary obligation to him in the matter of the premium, which could only be discharged in one way; for, to judge by the appearance of her father, he had come back even poorer than he had left England. Well, she would now be able to help him as well as the rest —four of them, instead of three—that was all.

Still it was a relief to her that not a word was spoken about the man the thought of whom was ever present with her, and shadowed her young life with gloom and evil presage. In vain she had called up every argument to strengthen his cause, and back the claim she felt to be unanswerable: his solicitude for her and his; his generosity; his patience and forbearance. The very constancy with which he clung to her, and pursued her, ranged itself upon the other side, and increased her sense of repugnance—nay, of loathing.

It was a part of the plan agreed upon between Dalton and Philip that they should say no more for the present about Holt and his transactions than they should be absolutely obliged to say; and it surprised them both to find how easy it was to maintain their reticence. Neither Kitty nor Jenny asked their father one word about the *Lara,* nor put a question respecting his pecuniary affairs. It is true they had taken it for granted that matters were the reverse of prosperous with him, which would have been a sufficient reason for avoiding the subject; but in any case—poor though they were, and suffering from the ills of poverty—such material woes were for the moment forgotten in the joy of seeing him back again.

"I think I have reason to be proud of my darlings, Philip," said Dalton, as the two walked together with Jeff from Brown Street that night to the lodgings which that young gentleman had procured them near his own. "I had ruined them, and as it must have seemed to them" (he pointed to his shabby coat) "had failed in saving anything from the wreck of their fortunes, yet not a syllable have they spoken to me upon the subject, lest, doubtless, it should sound as a reproach."

"I expected nothing less," answered Philip quietly. "I feel several inches higher since those two girls have called me uncle. They have nothing sordid about them, such as I, alas! have seen in my fellow-creatures all my life."

"And it isn't as if they had not to think of shillings and pence," put in Jeff eagerly. "If you could know how Kitty has cut and contrived, and striven to make both ends meet, during the last six months——" .Here he stopped, for a look of intense pain came into Dalton's face.

" Well, well ; that will be all over now, I trust, Jeff. To-night we have still to do some dirty work, and then we shall have clean hands for the future ; we will avoid rogues and fair-weather friends, and all worthless folk, and my dear ones shall have no further cause for tears. I think Jeff should know what we are going to do with respect to Holt, Philip."

Their plan of attack, unfolded to their young friend at their lodgings, was simple enough.

A letter was to be posted to Holt that night informing him that his fraud respecting the *Lara* mine was discovered ; and that his malpractices respecting other affairs of Dalton, of which he had had the management, was more than suspected. Restitution was imperatively demanded ; and, in default of it, he was assured that criminal proceedings would at once be instituted. There were no upbraidings ; but a more curt, decisive, and stern epistle was never penned.

Philip would have preferred that their opinion of Holt's treachery should have been stated in

Saxon English; but Dalton would not have it.
Such a course, he thought, would have taken for
granted a certain familiarity to still exist between
him and this scoundrel, of whose connection with
himself he felt unspeakably ashamed.

"What makes me mad with him," said Philip,
"is to think he should have dared to lift his eyes
towards Kate. Such vermin ought to be poisoned
out of hand. What do you say, Jeff?"

"I am bound to say," returned the young fellow
gravely, "that Mr. Holt—whatever may have been
his reasons for it—has been considerate, and even
kind to me."

"But you are not going back to him, surely,
after *this*?" said Philip in amazement.

"Well, yes; I shall go to-morrow, for the last
time. He may have something to urge, I do not
say in excuse, but in extenuation of his roguery.
Your letter gives him no opportunity for this."

"Opportunity, indeed!" rejoined Philip, with
irritation. "I would send him a rope, to afford
him the opportunity of extenuating himself on
that. If you get talking with that wily scoundrel,
my young friend, you will be wound round his little
finger."

"Our Jeff—being honest—contends at a disadvantage with most people," observed Dalton, laying his hand on the young fellow's shoulder; " yet in the end I should be inclined to back him. Let him take his own way, and we will take ours."

Accordingly, Jeff went to Abdell Court next morning, as usual. Mr. Holt had not arrived; nor, said the office boy, had he yet returned from the country. Upon his table was lying the usual pile of letters, which it was Jeff's business to sort and dispose of. Some he was empowered to open and answer; some he would open only and make an "abstract" of for his employer; others he would put aside for his private eye. Among these last was one in Dalton's handwriting, with the contents of which, however, Jeff was already acquainted.

Eleven, twelve o'clock passed, and yet Mr. Holt came not. It would not have been surprising had his real destination of yesterday been what he had pretended it to be; but Jeff was well convinced that he had not gone to Plymouth, but to Liverpool, and there was now ample time for him to have gone and returned. At one o'clock the office closed for an hour, during which Holt was accustomed to deny himself to everybody, whether he was within doors or not; and a little before one he

came. He looked jaded, wan, and pale, like one
who had been on a toilsome expedition, and failed
in its proposed object—or so it seemed to Jeff, who
observed him narrowly—but there was no other
change in his appearance, no cowed or defiant looks,
such as might have been expected had he known
that Dalton had landed upon English soil. Jeff
felt sure he did not know.

"Well, what news, Mr. Derwent? Who has
been?"

"Mr. Dawkins called just after you went away
yesterday, and appeared to wish to see you very
much."

"What about?" inquired Holt quickly. "But
it's no matter. It was most likely about that
cock-and-bull story about the *Flamborough Head.* I
daresay you have heard it yourself, Mr. Derwent?"

"I have heard that some one—two persons
indeed—have been saved from the wreck."

"Well, it's true, for a wonder: Jones and Norton
are their names. I am sorry to say their story
destroys the last gleam of—— What's this?"
He had been sorting the letters with his hand,
and presently came upon the one despatched from
Islington the previous night. "What's this!"
he reiterated, in a voice grown suddenly hoarse and

low. "How did it come? Where did it come from?"

"It came by the early post, sir."

"It's strange," said Holt, with an air of indifference; "quite curious. Have you ever seen a handwriting like that? It reminds me of one who certainly never could have written it; and yet it gave me quite a turn. You know whom I mean, I daresay?"

He did not attempt to open the letter, and the strong, huge hand that held it in its grasp shook like a leaf.

"I know whom you mean," said Jeff, gravely. "It is Mr. Dalton's."

"Yes; it is like John Dalton's writing."

"It *is* his writing, sir."

"That is impossible; that is ridiculous. The post-mark disproves that. But there is a curious similarity, without doubt. Has the boy gone to his dinner?"

Jeff answered that he was; and Holt moved to the door and locked it.

"Now tell me, Mr. Derwent," said he, still toying with the letter—"for you are one who tells the truth—what makes you fancy that it was really Dalton who wrote this? As a matter of fact, as I

have already stated, there were but two men saved
from the wreck of the *Flamborough Head*."

"1 know it, Mr. Holt: they were John Dalton
and Philip Astor."

"That's a lie!—that's a lie!" exclaimed the other,
passionately. "You are a liar, like the rest;" but
his pale face belied his words; he staggered rather
than sank into his chair.

"You had better open the letter, and see who is
the liar," said Jeff, haughtily.

"You speak of Astor, but you don't know the
man as I do," continued Mr. Holt. "He is an utterly
untrustworthy and contemptible fellow. He was
here once, in your place; and I trusted him too far,
and he repaid me for my confidence by forgery.
He is not to be believed upon his oath. If
there is anything in this letter founded upon his
evidence——"

"You had surely better read it, Mr. Holt," said
Jeff, curtly. He could not but feel some pity for
this miserable wretch, who evidently dreaded the
thing he held in his quivering fingers as though it
were a very adder.

"What! you know its contents, then?" exclaimed
the other sharply. "You are in the conspiracy
with Astor and the rest. You think it honest, do

you, to take your wages here, and turn against the hand that pays them?"

"I know what is in that letter, Mr. Holt; but yet I am no conspirator," answered Geoffrey steadily. "On the contrary, I came here to-day—for the last time—to do what good I could for you. As for your wages, they were paid for work, I suppose; or if that was overpaid, you had your reasons for it; but I owe you thanks for civil treatment, and I am here to give them."

Holt had opened the letter by this time, and ran his eye through its half-dozen pregnant lines.

"It is not Astor's word Mr. Dalton has taken, you see, sir," continued Jeff, "but the evidence of his own senses. He has been to Brazil, and seen the *Quito*. As for the other matters, you know best; but——"

"Ay, it is all over," murmured the other. "It is no use holding on to a falling stock, Mr. Derwent, eh? That's one of the great principles of our business." Holt was looking at Jeff, and speaking to him, yet he seemed almost unconscious of his presence. His eyes had no speculation in them; his tones were mechanical. Presently he cried out, like one who is wrung with a sharp physical pain: "Does Kitty know of all this, Jeff?"

CHAPTER XVII.

MR. HOLT MAKES JEFF HIS CONFIDANT.

UNDER ordinary circumstances, Mr. Holt could scarcely have made an observation so displeasing, and calculated to set his companion at odds with him, as that most unexpected one with respect to Kitty; but the tone in which it was uttered, and the look that accompanied it, disarmed the young fellow altogether; nay, more, it filled his soul with compassion for this beaten wretch. For if ever a man looked beaten in the battle of life, not at one point, but at all, and not only beaten, but broken and utterly despairing, it was the once prosperous, and demonstratively prosperous, Richard Holt.

"Does Kitty know of all this, Jeff?"

The use of the two familiar names was most significant, since they comprised not only a confession of hopeless love, but an appeal to the generosity of his rival. "Tell me," it seemed to say, "for mercy's sake, if I am lost in the eyes of her I love, as well as in those of the rest of the world; or whether, so far as she is concerned, I can still hold up my head? I appeal to you, because your heart is kind and sound, and you are one neither to lie to me, nor, though I am helpless and fallen, to tread me under foot."

" Kitty does not know, Mr. Holt—as yet," answered Jeff hesitatingly.

"And yet *you* know, and did not tell her!" put in the other quickly. "There are few men in your case who would have waited so long. Her father, however, has perhaps informed her this morning?"

"No, Mr. Holt; it was arranged that she is to be told nothing till he has had your reply to his letter."

" Then I will give him his reply," answered the other calmly. He opened a little box that lay on his office desk, and took from it a sheet of figures. " Here is my account with John Dalton," said he, " which you can presently examine at your leisure. He will find that I was a more honest man than he took me for—up to yonder date," pointing it out with his finger. "The *Lara* itself was a *bonâ fide* investment in the first instance. He and I both made money out of it, and would have continued to do so legitimately, but for my passion for the girl you love. That was what drove me to my ruin. Ah, you do not comprehend that! If you loved her, as I did—and as I do—it would be easier for you to understand it.—Nay, forgive me. I was wrong there. An honest love doubtless takes honest ways, and only those, to win its object. Call mine dishonest, then, if you will; yet it was genuine of its sort, believe me. Its nature was devouring, and I denied it nothing—honour, reputation, self-respect, were all thrown into that flatal flame. From the first moment that I beheld her, I swore to make that girl my wife; and now I shall die perjured." He smiled a wretched smile, and sighed, then wearily went on : " Her father would have none of me. He had opened the doors of his house to me with reluctance, and I found no favour there. In vain I worked for him and enriched him. When I ventured upon ever so slight an approach to familiarity with those belonging to him, he took no pains to conceal his annoyance— his astonishment at my presumption. I had some pride of my own also, and this wounded me to the quick. Since I had no chance to attain my object while he was prosperous, I resolved to ruin him."

Jeff uttered an exclamation of disgust.

"I am sorry to offend you, Mr. Derwent; but this is a relation of facts. The last dying speech and confession of a man under the gallows, you know " (here he smiled again, if possible more

ghastlily than before), "and does not concern itself
with sentiment. I had tried fair means to no purpose; and I was not to be balked. I could not bend
John Dalton, so I resolved to break him. Hitherto,
he had been, practically speaking, my partner in
all the business we transacted with one another;
now I made him unconsciously my confederate. I
set rumours afloat about the *Lara,* which brought
down the shares, and then I bought them up. In
the end, Dalton and I possessed the mine between
us, though I told him afterwards that I had parted
with all my interest in it. Whatever we had now
to do in concert, I secured the lion's share of profit
for myself—it is all there" (he pointed to the
schedule) "in black and white—not because I was
grasping, but because I wished to dock his gains.
When there was loss, it was he who chiefly suffered. I fed his ambition, and encouraged him
to make a figure in politics as well as commerce;
knowing that politics would cost him money and
not fill his pocket, as they do with some men.
When funds began to fail him, I matured my
scheme concerning the mine. I sent a creature of
my own (the 'expert' Tobbit) to Brazil, to report
upon the *Lara*—to the English shareholders (in
reality to Dalton and myself), with instructions to
declare it valueless; with what success you know.

Still I could not get Dalton to dispose of his shares: some influence was at work—I now feel certain it must have been that of Astor — to induce him to hold them. His resolve to go to Brazil to look into matters for himself filled me with dismay, yet I strove in vain to hinder him. When he had once embarked, it was, I knew, but a question of a few months, and then my fraud would be exposed. But if I could only have secured Kitty in the meantime, that would not have disturbed me. To that end I applied every means in my power; but though I had a keen ally in Mrs. Campden, I made no progress. You will learn all that from other sources. You know, even though the *Flamborough Head* went down, and Fortune seemed to favour me to the uttermost, and to turn her back upon those weak ones with whom I warred, that I was never Kitty's accepted suitor."

Jeff was not quick at figures, but he could calculate better than any man what it cost his defeated rival to say those words. And yet even he knew not their full meaning. This unhappy wretch was not all evil (as some of us are, I fear, in spite of some philosophic observers who have reported to the contrary); since he could not marry Kitty himself, he was willing that the man who might, and who certainly deserved to do so, should be quite clear in his own mind that his wife had never plighted troth—no matter under what circumstances—to another; he was willing that this should be, and he was above measure desirous that Kitty in accepting Jeff should on her part feel uncompromised as respected himself. It was not all generosity—though people can afford to be generous when making their wills; he was solicitous that his memory at least should not be odious to Kitty.

"Do I speak plainly, Mr. Derwent?" said Holt, after a short pause.

"You are giving yourself unnecessary pain, sir," answered the young fellow kindly; "as for me, I am but a messenger to carry back to those who sent me your acceptance of certain terms."

"That is true; but confession, they say, is good for the soul, and I prefer you to any priest, Jeff." He was right there, so far, at all events, as making his peace in this world was concerned. He knew that in that young and generous nature he should find such an apologist as he would have looked for in vain elsewhere; and that apologist would have the ear of her whose censure or contempt alone had terrors for him. "As for the terms you speak of," he went on, "I have no choice but to accept them. The figures I have given you will show my indebtedness to Mr. Dalton, to which the interest shall be added. The calculation will take a little time—perhaps a few hours; may I ask, until they have expired, that this "—here his face showed a tinge of colour—" this matter of business may not be spoken of, save among those to whom it is already known ? "

" So far as I have any influence, Mr. Holt, you may depend—— "

" I ask no more, save one thing," interrupted the other with a wave of his hand; the first recurrence he had made to his favourite continental manner. " Though easily granted, it is a great favour, but it is the last I shall ever seek from you. You hesitate to pledge yourself beforehand," added he with a faint smile: " that is only natural under the circumstances. However, this little matter can be performed ' without prejudice,' as the lawyers say : there is no dishonesty in it, I assure you ; no harm to any one, but some good, or at least some pleasure to me, whose pleasures are mostly come to an end."

" I will do it, sir," said the young fellow, simply.

" Then good-bye, Jeff; and may your life be a brighter and a better one than mine has been."

" But the favour, sir ? " said the young fellow, greatly moved.

" Oh, it was merely that—that you would shake

hands with me." He did so. "After all that has come and gone, I was more than doubtful whether you would. It cost you something, Jeff, I saw; but in the end you will not repent it."

Then resuming his usual business manner, he added: "John Dalton will receive all his dues by to-morrow morning at latest; and your salary will be sent to you, up to this date, by the same post. I am sorry that circumstances have caused us to part company, Mr. Derwent; but needs must when the devil drives, and he was certainly the coachman in this case. As for to-day I have much business of a private nature to arrange, and have no further occasion for your services."

As he said those words, he sat down, and took up his pen; Geoffrey bowed and left the room, and in a few minutes the office. His leave-taking had been altogether different from anything he could have imagined, and puzzled him, now that it was over, even more than during its occurrence. The tone and manner of the speaker had seemed to explain much at the time, but now they were absent, his memory failed to supply them; the lights of the picture were wanting, and the impression it produced upon him was one of unmitigated gloom.

Its tints would have been darker yet if he could have looked—but a few hours—into the future.

CHAPTER XVIII.

HOW MR. HOLT HASTENED MATTERS.

In spite of all that had happened to the family in whom Geoffrey Derwent had so large an interest —the return of Dalton, his recovered wealth, which would once more reinstate those belonging to him in their former position; and his own prospects, which had altered so materially for the worse (for the "opening" which he had looked for in business was now closed, and the gulf between him and Kitty yawned as wide as ever)—in spite of all these important considerations, Jeff's mind, as he turned his steps towards Islington, was mainly occupied with his late employer. Notwithstanding all the villainy to which he had confessed, the young fellow's heart was pitiful towards him; not a word of sorrow for his delinquencies against Dalton had passed his lips, though he had promised material reparation; but on the other hand his sensitiveness as respected Kitty had been extreme.

It was for her—though selfishly—that he had
sinned—had gone through the fire of shame and
the foul water of fraud; and Jeff's own great love
for her—though it would never have thus led *him*
astray—made excuses for his rival. He pictured
him during those weeks when Dalton had first
sailed from England, and he must have been
expecting day by day the tidings of the exposure
of his crime, and pitied him. It was perhaps
pity misplaced, for Holt was a man with nerves of
iron; a man, too, of means and subtle device,
whom the law could not have thrown on his back
like a turtle (as it throws the poor and dull who
transgress it) to await trial and sentence; but
judging his case by what his own would have been
in the like conditions, and also taking into consideration the fact that the man was down, and
harmless, Jeff, on the whole, was glad that he had
given him the hand, not indeed of friendship, but
forgiveness.

Jeff's day was all his own—as many days to
come were, alas! likely to be—yet he hesitated to
visit Brown Street, where of late he had been so
unwelcome. Moreover, he feared that he should
be subject to questioning there upon the events of
the day, which recent experience warned him that
he was not fitted to undergo; he entertained the

just conviction that Jenny would have "turned him inside out" (as they say at the Old Bailey) in five minutes of cross-examination. He resolved to go, therefore, to Dalton's lodgings, and there leave a line to state the result of his interview with Holt, with that proviso added as to "the date of publication" of it, and then pass the time as he could till evening. He found, however, a note at the house awaiting him, asking him to come on to Brown Street to dinner; an invitation which he had not the courage—or the cowardice—to refuse.

He found the family all in high spirits, with one exception. Dalton, indeed, was not so debonair and joyous as he had been wont to be; his manner had something of sardonic exultation, in place of its old *abandon*, and it became him less. He had been hard hit, and he was a man not used to blows; such men return them with interest, and feel a pleasure in the repayment. A rapid glance had passed between him and Jeff, which assured him that his enemy was vanquished. Jenny, bright, gay, and frail as a bird, was full of fun, with every now and then a dash of spleen amidst her sprightliness, like a sparrow turned sparrow-hawk; she had been hit too (for was not each slight a blow to one so fragile?), and was not one to forget it. The sudden change for the better in the

sick girl showed how much mental trouble and
material privations had had to do with her malady.
Tony was in tearing spirits, now dancing about his
father, now romping with Uncle Philip, whom he
had taken to as naturally as though he had been a
member of the family from the first. Only Kitty
was not merry: when her face was turned towards
her father or Jenny, it beamed indeed with smiles;
a sense of gratitude seemed to environ her like an
atmosphere; but she was strangely silent, and
when not addressed had a grave and quiet look,
that reminded one more of resignation than con-
tentment. Perhaps, Jeff dared to hope, she had
been reflecting, like himself, that the course of true
love was not likely to run smoother than of yore
with them; that this new-found prosperity, while
it made self-sacrifice unnecessary, would still be a
fatal obstacle to her heart's desire. For that she
knew that she was once more prosperous, was
certain. The air of the whole party convinced
him that such was the case, and especially the air
of good Nurse Haywood, who waited upon them at
dinner in person, and treated "Master John," as
she still persisted in calling Dalton, like a prince
who has not only returned to his native land, but
come back to enjoy his own again. He would
have had of her best as long as it lasted—had he

been a beggar, but her behaviour would in that case have been less unlike a prolonged flourish of trumpets. Indeed, it might be said that there were cymbals also, for in her excitement and exultation she clashed the plates together and broke a couple.

"It doesn't matter, if there are enough left to go round," said Dalton.

"Thank heaven, it doesn't, Master John," answered the old lady; "for there are plenty *now* where those came from."

She had got some bottles of champagne from the public-house, the whole of which she would have dispensed to the company, and thereby have poisoned them, for the Brown Street vintage was execrable.

"I am afraid you don't like it, sir," said she aggrieved; "but it was the best I could get at such a short notice."

"The wine is excellent, nurse," said Dalton gravely; "but one bottle is quite sufficient to drink the health of all *our* friends in."

The list of toasts, indeed, was short enough. They drank Dr. Curzon's health; and, in spite of her remonstrances, they drank to Nurse Haywood herself, the men shaking hands with her, and the two girls overwhelming her with caresses. It would certainly have been no exaggeration had she observed in acknowledgment, that it was the proudest moment of her life; her only reply, however (and how far preferable would it be if after-dinner acknowledgments in general took that form), was a flood of tears.

When the ladies had retired, taking Tony the reluctant (who, so far from finding fault with the Brown Street champagne, had done ample justice to it) with them, Dalton laid his hand on Geoffrey's shoulder.

"And now, lad, for your news from Abdell Court. I need not ask if it be good news, for I have read so much as that already in your face."

"Yes, sir; it *is* good news. Mr. Holt admits all that is urged against him, and promises to make the completest reparation; only for a few hours—the time he named, indeed, must have elapsed by now—he begged to be spared exposure."

"What did the fellow mean?" inquired Dalton angrily. "Did he want to shut my mouth, if a man had asked me any time to-day, is Richard Holt a villain?"

"I think he merely meant that until you had heard from him this evening, he hoped you would not make his shame known to your own family."

"My family!" echoed Dalton scornfully. "The scoundrel has small claim to forbearance as respects them, I reckon. Do you know, man," added he with stern solemnity, "that it is thanks to him that my dear wife is lying in her grave at Sanbeck ? "

It was certainly true that through Holt's fraud, Dalton had been forced to leave the country, and that out of his absence had arisen the catastrophe at the Nook.

Jeff hung his head ; the argument had gone home to him ; he felt he had nothing more to say for the unhappy wretch, whose hand he had taken that day for the last time.

" Come," said Dalton; "let us not think of villains to-night. There was one toast, Jeff, I didn't propose while the girls were here, because I wished to save your blushes; but I mean to drink it now. Philip, fill your glass; the sherry, I think, is a little less deadly than that champagne. As good wine needs no bush—if the converse be true, by-the-bye, this wine should require a thicket—so a toast that we drink with all our hearts needs no speech. My toast is Geoffrey Derwent. You don't know him, Philip, as I know him (nor did I know him, for that matter, as I ought to have known him, till within the last two days). But you may take my word for it, that young as he is, a truer heart, or one more to be relied upon, in times that try men's hearts and show what stuff they are made

of, does not beat than his. I need not repeat the
story; but Jenny has told me all about you, Jeff;
and if Kitty has told me nothing, there has been,
I daresay, some very good reasons for her silence.
I have no secrets from Philip here, not even that
one; and I have a particular object in saying what
I have to say before Philip. His notion is, that
with returning prosperity, I shall fall into the old
tracks; that ' the deceitfulness of riches '——"

" I never said so, John," interrupted Philip; "I
only thought——"

"Well, you see, he *thought* it," put in Dalton
quickly, " and that is quite as bad. To put the matter
beyond question, however, so far as you are concerned, Jeff, I wish, in Philip's presence, to remind
you of a certain confession you made to me with respect to Kitty, when you and I parted company at
Riverside. Do you remember what it was, Jeff?"

" Yes, indeed; I remember very well, sir."

"And do you recollect what I said to you in reply?"

" You said you would talk to me about that
when you came back again."

" Very good; and now, you see, I am keeping
my promise. Well, if you still love Kitty, and she
loves you, she is yours, Jeff ! "

" Oh sir, you are too good !" cried Jeff, his heart
bounding with joy and gratitude, though conscious

s 2

of a doubt. " But, alas! I have nothing; and Kitty
will be rich; and people will say——"

" Let them say what they like, and be hanged! "
cried Dalton vehemently. " If ' people '—by which
I suppose you mean one's friends—would say a
little less, and do a little more, when occasion
demands it, their opinion would be of more
consequence." He pushed his chair back from
the table, and began walking up and down the
little room as he went volubly on : " It has always
of course been acknowledged of Society, even by
the prosperous, that she was ' frivolous ' and
' hollow,' and all that sort of thing ; but I could
not have imagined, unless I had experienced
it myself, how worthless and rotten at the core
the creature is. The women are worse than the
men, because they protest so much. To think of
the scores of them that have smirked and smiled,
and asked me after my ' dear girls ' with such
tender sympathy; and then, when one's back was
turned—as they thought for good—and these same
' dear ' ones were left helpless and penniless, how not
one—not *one* of these fine folks would hold a finger
out, or even say a word of comfort! No, Jeff; don't
talk to me of what ' people ' may ' say,' or I shall
be tempted to think that those who are not knaves
in the world must needs be the other thing."

Philip sat back in his chair, jingling some halfpence in his pocket—probably all the money he
had—and very much applauding these remarks;
but a keener observer would perhaps have had
a suspicion that Dalton was working himself up
to this display of vehemence, or, at all events,
found it necessary to nurse his wrath in order
to keep it warm. The fact was, not only was his
nature eminently genial, and inapt for receiving
deep impressions, especially of an unpleasant sort,
but second nature—use—had made him regard the
very class of persons he was now anathematising, as
his own world, beyond which he had few sympathies.
His feelings, however, with respect to Geoffrey Derwent were genuinely what he described them to be,
and he was perfectly honest in the offer he had just
made him of his daughter's hand.

"Perhaps you would like to go upstairs, my
lad, and have a few words with Kitty," added he
kindly, "while we old fellows smoke a cigar;" as he
spoke he threw open the window, admitting a little
air, a good deal of dust, and the growing chorus
of some street hawkers, who at that period of the
evening were wont to "work" Brown Street, and
supply it with the latest sensational intelligence.

Jeff smiled his thanks, and left the room; but
his step on the narrow staircase was not that of a

lover who has "asked papa" with success; and on the landing he paused for full a minute, weighing this and that, in most unlover-like fashion; for, with all his good qualities—among which a loving heart was not certainly wanting—Jeff was intensely proud. His darling hope had been, if only circumstances had permitted it, that he might have made for himself some position in the world—humble but not despicable, and such as he could have lifted Kitty out of her difficulties to share.

In wedding her as things were, he would not indeed be marrying her for money; but the inequality in their fortunes jarred upon his sensitive feelings. Among such natures—for low ones find no difficulty in the matter—it requires a strong mind and an exceptionally wholesome one to accept a pecuniary obligation without repugnance. The worship of money is so well-established, that even those who ought to know it is an idol are apt to treat it as a sacred thing.

In the drawing-room he found Kitty seated close to her sister, with the latter's arm about her waist. It was generally Jenny who "did the talking" when they were alone together, and she had evidently been doing it on this occasion. Kitty had the downcast looks of a listener who has been preached at.

"Talk of Jeff, and he makes his appearance!" said Jenny, saucily.

"I hope I am not intruding?" observed he humbly.

"You are intruding on *me*, sir," said Jenny, rising from her chair. "I have had quite enough of you below-stairs for the present;" and off she tripped, leaving the two young people alone. The window was open here, as in the room below, but the dust was less, and the wind that passed over the flower-box on the sill brought charming odours with it.

"Kitty, dear, your father has been speaking to me most kindly," said Jeff, hesitatingly.

"He is always kind, and in your case can never, I am sure, be otherwise, Jeff," answered she steadily. "He knows that he owes you very much."

"I don't feel that, Kitty; but I feel that whatever he owes me, or can owe me, it can never be so much by a hundred times as what he says he is prepared to give me. Can you guess, Kitty, darling, what that is?"

"Jeff—Geoffrey," said she, in distressed tones, "did you not promise at the Nook——"

"Yes, dear," interrupted he; "but that was different. The circumstances are altogether changed. They are not indeed as I could wish them to be, even yet. I am poor, I may say penniless, when compared with you——"

"Oh Jeff, how dare you!" exclaimed Kitty, rising angrily from her seat. "Do you suppose I am thinking of money? Of course, I have had to think about it of late—for others; but in a matter that concerns myself alone, can you think that your being poor or rich can draw me, by a hair's-breadth, one way or another?"

"It draws *me*, Kate," cried Jeff simply. "It is the only thing that draws me—just a hair's-breadth—away from you. I thought, when I spoke to you at the Nook, that it was the reflection how ill off we both were as respected means; and that, in your unselfishness and generosity, you felt it right to be the prop and stay of your own household, and not to look outside of it, even for such love as mine."

"It was partly that, Jeff; but also, even then, there was another contingency, and that, alas!—the other obstacle, I mean—has grown and grown; indeed, I don't know how I stand respecting it. I—I—you must please to give me time, Jeff; and I can't promise; indeed I can't."

"But you have promised no one else, Kitty?"

"No; at least not exactly; but——"

The shouting of the hawkers in the street was growing nearer and nearer: as one on one side, and one on the other, they bawled together, like singers in a glee who are out of tune, it needed a practised ear to catch a word.

"This noise is dreadful," muttered Jeff; and

moving quickly to the window, he pulled down the sash and shut out the sound.

"You need time, Kitty, to think it over," said Jeff softly; "well, let it be so; I was not impatient, you know, before."

It was not impatience, nor yet disappointment, nor distress, that agitated the speaker; yet his face had blanched, and wore an expression anxious and *distrait.* But Kitty's eyes were fixed upon the floor, and saw him not.

"No; you were patient, and good, and kind as you ever were, Jeff," answered she, tenderly. "Whatever happens, I shall always think of you as—as all that. But indeed I must have time."

"I am going now," said Jeff, and indeed his hand was already on the door. Never surely were two fond lovers so willing that time and space should separate them, as these two seemed to be.

Throughout the day, from the moment her father had told her better times had come to them—he could no longer deny himself that pleasure, though he had forborne to speak of how his fortune was about to be restored to him—Kitty had been revolving in her mind her position as respected Holt. The money that he had advanced for the life-insurance premium would now be repaid to him of course, but could that acquit her of her obligation?

and if it did, would it release her from the implied though unexpressed consent she had given to accept of his attentions? It was easy to break with him indeed, but could it be done with a good conscience? In her heart of hearts, Kitty knew she had made up her mind to marry this man, and she feared that he knew she had done so. To marry him now —all the forces that had driven her towards him having suddenly ceased to exert their influence, while the dead-weight of dislike still drew her in the opposite direction—she felt to be impossible; but she also felt, notwithstanding the arguments which Jenny had just been pouring into her ear, and the still stronger claims which love itself, in the person of Jeff, was urging, that much, very much was owed to Richard Holt; indeed that all was owed by rights, only that the debt was too excessive for payment. At all events it was for him to impose what terms he pleased in default of its discharge. Until she had confessed to him that notwithstanding all that had come and gone she could never be his wife, she felt at least that it was unbecoming to speak of marriage with another. Hence it was she had said: "I must have time."

And Jeff needed "time" too, though for a very different purpose. He could not understand her scruples, for had not Mr. Holt himself said: "I have wooed her without success;" yet he felt confident that the obstacle to which she had alluded was Holt, and no other. He was not at liberty—or did not feel himself to be so—to say that this man had already renounced his claim, if claim he had upon her; but something had suddenly taken place which might set her at liberty another way. And yet, to do Jeff justice, it was not that thought which was paramount in his mind as, having quitted the presence of his beloved Kitty, he flew downstairs, and snatching up his hat, let himself softly out of doors. Through the open window on his left he could hear Dalton and his half-brother talking earnestly over their cigars; he even caught the name of "Holt" coupled with some adjective, expressive of contempt and loathing: it was strange, considering what he knew of the man, that he should feel pained to hear it; but so it was.

Then turning to the right hand, he sped away after the two street hawkers, who, having cried themselves hoarse, were just about to enter the public-house at the corner, to refresh themselves with purl—a liquor as popular with gentlemen of *their* calling as Dublin stout is said to be with our fashionable sopranos.

"I want a copy of your paper; quick!" he said, as he came up with them.

"Well, you see, sir, it's the last we have," grumbled the man addressed; "and I don't think as sixpence is too much——"

Jeff threw him a shilling and snatched the newspaper out of his hands, unconscious of the muttered remark of the vendor's partner: "Why didn't you ask the bloke a suverin for it?" He was a political economist of the soundest type, and had seen the necessity, which the other had omitted to see and take advantage of.

Jeff's practised eye lighted at once upon the big letters—"Suicide Extraordinary in Abdell Court."

He had caught the name as he had sat at the open window, though it had escaped the ears of those who were less familiar with it, and at once associated the catastrophe with his late employer. His air and manner during their late interview were quite in consonance with such a deed, and even (as he now thought) his shameless candour. Had not the wretched man himself likened it to a confession at the gallows' foot!

Within five hours or so of Jeff's parting with him at the office, Richard Holt had blown out his brains.

CHAPTER XIX.

HOW THEY LIVED EVER AFTERWARDS.

JEFF crumpled the newspaper into his pocket, and walked back in haste to the house he had just quitted. He would tell the news at once to Mr. Dalton, and then Kate would receive it, as it should be told, from her father's lips. He knew Dalton's nature too well to fear that he would feel or express any cruel exultation at the death of his enemy; but he was not prepared for the grave solemnity with which he received the intelligence.

"I have news, which I am sure you will both deem sad news," said Jeff as he closed the parlour-door behind him; "Mr. Holt is dead. He shot himself this afternoon in his office in Abdell Court."

"I am not surprised," said Philip coolly; "he was not a man to live disgraced."

Dalton said nothing for a minute or so. It was not mere pity that made him speechless; it was something more—a certain sympathy. His memory was recalling that scene on Bleabarrow crags when he himself had been about to appear unsummoned in the presence of his Maker. "Heaven have mercy on him, and forgive him, as I do!" were his first words.

"Poor devil!" said Philip, by way of epitaph, and as though the subject in its sentimental aspect were thereby dismissed and done with. "I hope we shall have no trouble in consequence of this, about the shares and things."

"He said he 'had much business of a private nature to arrange,'" said Jeff, "when I parted from him; and he had five hours of life before him then; I feel confident that they were spent in reparation."

"Let us hope for the best," said Philip; which, let us imagine, was a pious wish with regard to the dead man's future.

Then the two men began to talk, in quite a different manner than that they would have used half an hour before, of Holt's character. They both agreed that he was an excellent man of business: keen, diligent, and firm as a rock in a storm.

"If he had cared for anybody but himself, he might have been a happy man," was Dalton's verdict.

"You are wrong there, Mr. Dalton," said Jeff confidently. "He cared for Kitty."

"Hang his impudence!" said Philip. "Mind, I didn't say hang *him*."

Dalton frowned a little, but made no observation on the subject.

"Come," said he presently; "let us go up-stairs, and break it to the girls."

"If you will excuse me," said Jeff, "I would rather not see them again to-night."

"As you please, my lad," returned Dalton. "You had better look in at our place the first thing to-morrow morning. Come and breakfast with us, and then we can talk matters over."

Jeff accordingly went home at once, feeling that he had quite enough to think about, but only to find there more material for thought. At his lodgings he found a visitor who, his landlady informed him, had been awaiting his arrival there for hours; a certain Mr. Stretham, with whom, as Mr. Holt's confidential legal adviser, he had some slight acquaintance.

"You are surprised to see *me* here, no doubt, Mr. Derwent?" said this gentleman, in a tone which Jeff could not but consider was, under the circumstances, somewhat jaunty and indifferent.

"No, sir, I am not surprised," returned he, stiffly, "since I already know what has happened."

"The deuce you do! Mr. Holt led me to

understand that his intentions had not been disclosed to anybody. He sent me here with a most express injunction to see you to-night and communicate them."

" His intentions, sir? You cannot surely be referring to his design of committing suicide? Are you aware that he has blown his brains out ? "

" God bless my soul ! " cried the attorney, startled into devoutness. "You don't say so ! Blown his brains out ! and such clever brains, too ! Well, that explains the whole affair, then, which up to this moment has been so inexplicable to me. He has made over all his property by a deed of gift. If he had left it by will and then put an end to his life, don't you see there would have been a difficulty about the matter ? As it is, everything is quite simple. Even a verdict of *felo de se*—if a jury could be got to find it—would not affect the disposition of his money."

" I hope it has been so disposed, however, Mr. Stretham, independently of this deed of gift, that he has made restitution ? "

" Yes, yes ; we need not talk about that now. I guessed, of course, that there was something wrong —it was about that *Lara* mine, was it not? That money—every shilling of it—has all been paid, or is in course of payment."

"I am most sincerely pleased to hear it," said Jeff, with a sigh of relief. "It must be owned that he did what he could at last to put himself right with his fellow-men."

"Yes; and also to reward his friends," remarked Mr. Stretham, with significance.

"Indeed," answered Jeff, indifferently. "I was quite unacquainted with them; I knew nothing of his social relations."

"I don't know that he ever had any, except with Mr. Dalton, with whom it appears he has had disagreements. He has made over the whole of his property—something over fifty thousand pounds, I should say at a rough guess—to one Geoffrey Derwent."

"Left it to me!" exclaimed Jeff, astounded.

"Oh yes; there is no mistake about that. I was to remind you that he said you would have no reason to repent having shaken hands with him. I don't shake hands myself in a general way—I don't think it professional; but if I had thought my late client was so gratified by the ceremony, I would never have omitted it."

Jeff did not hear the pleasantry; his mind was occupied, not with his own accession to wealth, but with the difference of position in which it would place him as respected Kitty. Gratitude to the dead man, and gratitude also to Dalton, who had accepted him as his son-in-law without a penny, were contending in his heart. The former he could never repay; yet, strange to say, it affected him less of the two. It is the bane of the base that even their very gifts lack the savour of giving: moreover it must be remembered that Holt, having no further use for his money, must needs have given it to somebody. Afterwards, when Jeff came to think upon the matter, he felt the dead man's generosity more keenly, and acknowledged it in heartier fashion; for the conviction was borne in upon him—and it was no doubt a just one—that this vast fortune, given to himself, was, in fact, only given to him in trust to Kitty, who, as Holt had reflected, might have refused to accept it more directly.

On calling at Dalton's lodgings the next morning he found that Mr. Stretham had not exaggerated the completeness of his late client's settlement of all claims on his estate.

It appeared afterwards that throughout the progress of his frauds as respected Dalton, he had kept the most accurate debtor and creditor account of matters, and was thus enabled to repay every shilling—both principal and interest—in which he was indebted to him.

"If he could cook accounts, it must be owned,"

as Dalton observed afterwards, when the matter had grown familiar, "he could also keep them." He was, indeed, maugre a few grains of honest sentiment, a great financier, and admirably fitted to control the destinies of a joint-stock company or a foreign loan.

Kitty, I think, held another view of him, which —since he was dead and gone—almost took the form of tenderness. She understood the man, as regarded his affections, as only a woman could have done. She knew that when he had persecuted her most he had loved her as few men can love ; and now that he had become a mere memory, and she could, as it were, afford to do so, she in a manner respected him.

Even Jenny in days to come had a certain qualified praise for Mr. Holt, with whom she would frankly confess she " had had no patience until he left dear Jeff all that money." She thought there was more real good in him—if " grit " be good— than in such fair-weather friends as the Skiptons had proved themselves to be. She deemed him " worth a dozen " of such as Mrs. Campden ; but then, in Jenny's estimation, a dozen Mrs. Campdens were, to use a phrase of the auction-room, a very " cheap lot " indeed. He was a rogue, but at least he did not mingle his roguery with cant and " gush " and protestations of eternal friendship, wherein the word "eternal" had even a less extended sense than certain heretical theologians have of late attributed to it. These remarks, of course, are, however, like a Reuter's telegram, "in anticipation of our usual advices."

It may be easily imagined that as even Kitty's tender conscience had had little to urge against her union with Jeff as matters had stood, that she saw no obstacle to her own happiness, now that the other claimant for her hand had removed himself from the field; while whatever "people" might have "said" had the wedding taken place under other circumstances, they had now nothing but congratulations to offer upon the union between two young persons, not only so obviously fitted for one another, but whose means were so proportionate. It was every way a most "desirable" match; and was ever anything so "funny" as that father-in-law and son-in-law should possess the same diamond mine (or something) in Golconda (or somewhere) together! The whole thing seemed so "providential," as though it had been "preordained, as it were, you know."

Dalton went about saying the bitterest things against Society—and yet mixing in it almost as much as he had been wont to do. His smile was less genial, but his wit was even keener than of old. He was quite as much sought after as before, but not so well liked. It was complained of him by a great lady of fashion that Mr. Dalton would say " quite horrid things " at times ; by which it may be presumed her ladyship meant the naked truth. The fact was, Dalton was like a fish out of water among plain honest people, such as have no turn for epigram, who are content to keep their claret till the second day, and who use ready-made "dressing " for their salads. He knew that there were other atmospheres purer and more wholesome, and was angry with himself because he could not live in them ; or at least that they did not suit him. It is the fashion to say that adversity does us all good; but if it be so, John Dalton was an exception. His wife's death was a terrible loss to him. Doubtless such pure souls are well employed to whatever scenes of bliss they wing their flight; but to the post of guardian angel to her husband, which she had filled in this world to such perfection, there was no successor, and he missed her gracious influence sorely.

It must be said, however, to his credit, that notwithstanding her vacant chair at his fireside remained unoccupied, the sweet influences of home never lost their power over John Dalton.

After a sojourn at the seaside, which placed poor
Jenny at as good a standpoint in regard to health
as she had ever been, he took the family to the old
home in London which their mother's memory had
made so dear, and where a charming surprise
awaited them. Every article of furniture that
could be recovered from the purchasers at the sale
was found there in its old place; and the same
welcome and familiar faces greeted them, from
whom their father's Fallen Fortunes had at one
time compelled him to part.

The mistress of all indeed was absent; but
another member of the family was installed there
en permanence in the person of Uncle Philip.

Society, with her fine perception of what is right,
expressed herself as astonished and even "pained"
to perceive the landmarks of legitimacy thus
ignored; but she was not absolutely "outraged," as
she would have been had the *Quito* proved less
remunerative. She contented herself with hinting
that Mr. Dalton had doubtless his reasons for so
singular a proceeding; and that if everybody had
their rights, perhaps it would be found that the
case of Astor *versus* Dalton had been decided
wrongfully. The report was, that Philip had his
home and his income upon the understanding that
he did not marry, whereby complications might

arise to give employment to gentlemen of the long robe in the second generation; and the rumour received this much corroboration, that Philip remained a bachelor.

Jeff carried away his bride from her new old home at midsummer, but settled so near it, that Jenny and she were scarcely more apart than when they lived under the same roof. Her baby brother continued to be her especial charge and idol long after she had children of her own; and when many years after he followed his brother Tony's example and became an Eton boy, he received every "half" such hampers from Sister Kitty as to put to shame even the liberal contributions from his own home.

On the other hand, Tony and Jenny are as fast friends as ever; and though the former took a creditable degree at Cambridge, he has been heard to say, in the Society of Lincoln's Inn, that all that now remains to him in the way of learning which is worth a shilling was taught him by his second sister.

The chief guest at Kitty's wedding was Dr. Curzon; and I am afraid that the names of the company did not occupy a very long paragraph in *The Morning Post.* There were plenty of fine people who would have been glad to come, and I think Dalton would by that time have so far for-

given his fellow-creatures as to invite them; but
Kitty said: "No; if you please, papa; I would
rather have only real friends at my wedding."

It was very seldom she expressed herself with
such decision, yet somehow her husband was guided
by her in most things. "She has a very light
hand," Dalton used to say, "and Jeff has a tender
mouth." Above all things, Kitty had a horror of
"the City" and speculation of all kinds; and since
it would never have done for Jeff to be idle, she
sent him into Parliament, where he was greatly
liked. Though not distinguished for oratory, he
spoke now and then sensibly enough; and his opinion
upon commercial matters had some weight—at all
events in the smoking-room. It was generally
supposed there that he had been in early life
"largely connected" with the City. Very few
people know more of other people's early lives.
Curiously enough, it was never whispered that he
had been connected with literature. "His good
manners," Dalton said, "forbade the suspicion."

Jenny made quite a success as an authoress;
only her views were "dreadfully advanced," folks
said, "and her observations, really, you know, so *very*
severe." However, she put her principles, whatever they were, into practice, and aided with purse
as well as pen every genuine scheme of philan-

thropy if it only kept itself clear of patrons. She
did not like patronage even for other people, and as
for herself it was dangerous to offer it. A very
benevolent duchess who met Jenny on a Board once
tried it on with her, and is said to have been greatly
discomfited. Dalton's version of his daughter's
retort was that, shaking her curls and showing her
teeth at Her Grace like a Blenheim spaniel, she had
said: "Madam, don't *patronise me*, or I'll bite."

I am afraid Jenny has never forgiven Society for
its behaviour to her and hers, when they "went
under;" but on the other hand she does her best
to help and comfort those who are in the same sad
plight: for as to turning *her* back upon a friend—
she would as soon think of enlisting in the Horse
Guards. She was steadfast in all things, and from
one resolution nothing moved her—namely, that
she would never speak to Mrs. Campden. But for
her, perhaps, some sort of reconciliation would have
been patched up; as it was, the two families never
renewed their former intimacy. Mrs. Campden died
in a few years—of a cold, said the county paper,
caught in distributing tracts to " her poor people,
by whom she was greatly revered; " but strange to
say her loss brought Uncle George no nearer to his
old friends the Daltons. He knew that they har-
boured a bad opinion of his Julia, and a certain

chivalry of disposition forbade him to make advances to them.

In after-years indeed, Jeff and Kitty, with a whole tribe of pretty children, passed a summer month at Riverside; but the old geniality was wanting; Mr. Campden felt there was a subject, sealed, between them, yet one to which it was difficult not to make allusion.

He knew his wife had behaved ill, of course; but he made excuses for her—such as we know nothing about. Women, as everybody knows, will cling to their husbands, be they ever such scoundrels; and men will cling—though not so often— to wives who are mean and base, and make allowances for them such as astound the lookers-on.

Upon Jenny Dalton it was generally imagined that the plough of Adversity had made deep furrows, while her sister had remained unscathed, or that the marks of that rude discipline had soon worn away. But I venture to think that judgment was a superficial one. Kitty, like her mother, was a favourite in society, but—like her—the roots of all her happiness lay deep down in the garden-ground of Home. She forgave the world; but in her heart she never forgot its sorry treatment: she was gracious in return for its civilities; but she knew their value, and was not to be (twice) deceived.

Strange to say, her father, as I have hinted, was much more easily reconciled to his fair-weather friends, though he would sometimes gird at them.

"My darling," he once said to Kitty after a great reception at her house, and while he stood upon the hearth-rug, the last guest, previous to departure for the smoking-room of his club, "you have had a charming evening, and all these people have made themselves agreeable—or tried to do it; but don't be deceived by appearances : you had three or four hundred 'dear friends' here, but not half-a-dozen of them are really worth a button. You know we have tried it."

"Well, papa, I think we should make allowances. People neglected us when we were poor, no doubt; but no one—as a rule—acknowledges a claim which is founded only on sentiment ; or if they do, they soon get weary of satisfying it. Then, again, it is easy to say: 'If we had been in their place we should have acted very differently.' Perhaps we should, indeed I know we should; but *they* didn't know it. I have no doubt, excuses—such as appeared justifications—occurred to them very readily.".

"Nor I neither, my dear," laughed Dalton. "What I fear is, that, like your dear mother, you are so unsuspicious and so tender-hearted, that you take *au sérieux* (as poor Holt would have said) all these fine folks' professions. Now I believe that all the really good honest friends who would stand by one at a pinch can be counted upon the fingers of my two hands."

" Then, my dear papa, you are still very credulous," was Kitty's unexpected reply : " it has long been my conviction that the fingers of *one* hand would be amply sufficient for the computation."

THE END.

CHARLES DICKENS AND EVANS, CRYSTAL PALACE PRESS.